Airship 27 Productions

Strong Adventures

"The Hunt for the Cosmic Dagger," "The Mystery of the Voynich Manuscript," "The Journey Through the Vinland Veil," and "The Secrets of the Sky Temples" © 2024 Tyler Auffhammer

Published by Airship 27 Productions
www.airship27.com
www.airship27hangar.com

Cover and interior illustrations © 2024 Ron Hill

Editor: Ron Fortier
Associate Editor: Fred Adams Jr.
Marketing and Promotions Manager: Michael Vance
Production Designer: Rob Davis

ISBN: 978-1-953589-69-9

Printed in the United States of America

10 9 8 7 6 5 4 3 2 1

by Tyler Fluffhammer

TABLE OF CONTENTS

THE HUNT
FOR THE
COSMIC DAGGER

Egypt, 1922

"**G**rave robbers," murmured Harvey Strong, as he touched the wood-handled blade at his hip. He wore thick, black leather boots with his beige cotton pants tucked inside the boot shafts. His light blue shirt was uncommon among the others at the dig site, most likely because it was a New York brand and dye. Strong was an American, but it was not something that he wanted held against him. After all, he was working on an English dig site when Americans were just across the river. The English paid better, usually because they did things right, not just quickly.

On his shoulder sat a tri-colored ferret. The diggers called her *Haraami*, meaning "thief," in their Egyptian Arabic tongue. Strong had traded a single brass round for her in a local market a few weeks after he arrived. An assistant on the dig, Marc Lionel, tried to keep Strong from making the trade.

"She's a little thief, Strong," Lionel pleaded after watching the wiggling ferret stick her nose into his vest pockets.

Strong raised dogs in his youth, but never a ferret. He didn't want to take care of anything, but it was clear that this weasel's skills might come in handy at some point. He made the trade and now *Haraami* was his steadfast companion and a capable hunter, too. She had taken down three rabbits and numerous lizards since her arrival at camp.

Strong's gaze remained on the looters near the artifact tents. For weeks, these three vagrants—probably locals who needed the food to feed their families—had been making a mess of things at the dig. As head of dig site security, Strong decided against acting too hastily in taking out the looters. He watched them, waiting to see what they wore, what language they spoke, what they spoke of, and, of course, what they stole.

The three men were rummaging through artifact crates and it was obvious they didn't have experience as diggers because they left things more of a mess than when they found them. Each wore faded gray robes and a white turban. They were probably merchants whose businesses had failed after the excavations began. After all, the people don't need brass trinkets and rug dolls when there are mummies and gold necklaces to be found.

Strong stood from his seat beneath the open-ended canvas tent and grabbed his Henry repeating rifle that was leaning against the tent pole. It was a model that he had long employed in his line of work and this particular gun had been his for quite some time. Strong checked the volume of ammunition and, satisfied, began his march toward the artifact tents. Haraami rode on his shoulder, clinging with her claws to his blue shirt.

The dig had been going on for quite some time. How long exactly, Strong didn't know. He had arrived in Thebes from London nearly six months prior and didn't find the English loose with their information. What he did know was that a particularly fancy Lord Carnarvon, one of those dukes or earls in London, was getting frustrated with the meek artifacts that were sent from the dig in Thebes to his cool, plush English offices. Carnarvon was paying at least two different crews (that Strong knew of) to spend day after day pulling relics from the hot sand. There was Strong's crew, overseen by Dr. Kenneth Danby, an Egyptologist, and Howard Carter's group. With Carnarvon's anxiety at its head, there was now a crew digging night and day.

Luckily for Strong, his skills didn't suit the digger's life and he was assigned to dig site security. In the Great War, he was stationed with a mounted unit in Belgium. Like every other man, he had seen the atrocities of war, but left those memories with the dead men and boys in the field. The War didn't haunt him, like other men, because he had found a new purpose. As head of dig site security, Harvey Strong's sole purpose was to prevent "grave robberies, lootings, pillaging, or rapings to occur," according to Dr. Danby, on the day he had arrived in camp. Strong was not a zealous man, but did take his new position seriously. After all, the perks were some of the best in camp: a tent all his own, a decent wage, and the ability to drink liquor and carry guns as he wished. Most men in the camp were forbidden to drink or carry.

With the three looters in sight, Strong decided he was going to make an example out of them. If he did so now, it would likely keep others from taking their place, for a while. As he approached them, he raised the rifle to his hip and pointed it in their direction.

"Drop the goods and raise your filthy hands," commanded Strong, throwing in a menacing growl before each word. He was a naturally menacing figure, but was a decent actor, too.

As the three men dropped their canvas loot bags and raised their hands, their eyes tracked to their right. Strong followed their eyeline and found himself staring down the barrel of a Gewehr 98. He dove for cover behind a crate, just dodging a spray of bullets by the looters' henchman. In a panic, the looters grabbed all they could carry and made a mad dash toward their camel mounts.

Fairly safe behind the crate, Strong repositioned his curled-brim Stetson (the only in all Egypt) and cocked the lever of his rifle. Haraami had jumped from his shoulder in the midst of the gunfire and scampered behind a tent to safety. As the bullets from the Gewehr 98 riddled the crate with holes, it busted bottles of sweet wine that poured out of the breach. Strong tilted his head back, opened his mouth, and let the wine fill his gullet. With his wits about him, he slowly peered over the barrel to spot his antagonist. Immediately, the general vicinity of his head was littered with gunfire. He was stuck.

The gunfire had spooked the tiresome and underpaid diggers, who fled from the area in all directions. He had never seen the diggers run so fast. Usually, they loafed from dig site to dig site, never hurrying themselves unless a scorpion appeared beneath their feet. As Strong contemplated making his final stand, Mack Thatcher, right-hand man to Dr. Danby and a drinking companion of Strong, appeared from behind a cart full of stone.

Mack was firing a pair of Chamelot-Delvigne Model 1873 revolvers as he ran. The spray of fire from Mack's pistols quelled the gunfire from the looter henchman. Having spent all twelve rounds from Achilles and Hercules (as Mack referred to his pistols in his usual inebriated banter), Mack dove behind a nearby table, flipped it on its side for protection, and began reloading.

Mack's distraction allowed Strong to flee the quagmire. Strong jumped to his feet and trotted toward the tent his attacker had fled behind, rifle at the ready. When he realized the assailant was not going to make himself known, Strong's trot turned into a gallop and he ran toward the corral and the disappearing loot. Strong spotted the three grave robbers packing their saddlebags full of valuables and he hollered for them to stop where they stood. They slowly raised their hands, but were saved by another volley of gunfire from their henchman. Done with these games, Strong dropped onto one knee and took aim toward the henchman behind him, then let off a round from his rifle. The bullet struck the turbaned henchman in the shoulder, but the shot wasn't fatal.

In his regiment during the War, Strong had been nicknamed, "Good Enough," by Cpl. Stevenson, a high school teacher who recited poetry to the men during chow. Apparently, Strong had a knack for making shots that were "good enough" to put a man down, but not kill him. Strong didn't protest, but knew it was more than just dumb luck or blind shooting. He didn't enter the war to kill men. If a shoulder shot would have the same effect, it was worth a man's life. Rising to his feet, Strong cocked the rifle and prepared to subdue his attacker, but the sudden sound of a camel's gallop arose behind him.

Strong whipped around and saw the front legs of a large camel barreling toward him. The beast carried another looter henchman on his back, this one armed with a Mauser C96 and kilij. Before Strong could make a move, the camel and rider were upon him. The edge of the blade shone bright in the sunlight and Strong knew he was going to be a head shorter soon enough. Just in the nick of time, a barrage of bullets from Mack's reloaded pistols wounded the camel in the chest and it spilled its weight into the sand, sliding a few feet before its momentum died off. The unscheduled stoppage sent the rider end over end into the sand.

When the turbaned henchman rose to his feet, Mack kicked the pistol from his hand. The kilij was gone. Strong kicked the man in the belly, flipping the henchman onto his back. With one quick stroke, Strong placed the butt of his gun into the side of the man's head, knocking him out cold.

To their left, from behind a canvas tent, the other henchman appeared, his rifle working quickly through its clip. Mack dove to the right, careful not to scoop the sand with his pistol barrels. Strong dove to the left, rolled, and ended up on his belly with rifle pointed straight. He fired one shot, nicking the henchman in his left leg. The henchman fell to one knee, but kept firing back at them. The henchman's focus on Strong allowed Mack to flank the injured man. After a moment, Mack appeared behind him and placed his smoking pistols to the back of the man's head, close enough for him to smell the powder. The henchman dropped his rifle.

"Mack, watch these two while I retrieve our goods," Strong ordered, hopping the splayed out camel and sprinting toward the corral. Nodding agreeably, Mack struck the man in the back of the head with the butt of his pistol.

After a short jaunt to the corral, Strong realized the three camels and their riders were gone. In their place was a large canvas sack, devoid of the precious artifacts it once held. Strong threw his rifle sling over his shoulder and pulled a horse from the group in the corral. With no time to waste, he skipped the saddle, mounted the steed, and kicked it into a gallop with his boot heels.

The looters left behind a trail in the sand and Strong followed it east in the direction of a small village. There were a few large tents erected in the center of town. These were mining tents, Strong had come to learn. Mack, who had taken Strong under his wing the first day he arrived, told him that these were the tents where "men mined and gold was never found." Strong knew they were brothels, but liked the term "mining" much better. Around the tents were dozens of smaller ones—merchants mostly—along with a few sparse wooden shanties.

Strong slowed his horse when he entered the village to avoid arousing suspicion. Along the edges of the street, and sometimes in the middle, peddlers were selling their wares and people were trying to avoid them. It was a commercial free-for-all. An American businessman, Strong thought, with his resources and connections, could rule the capitalistic world if he had the determination and cunning of these Egyptian peddlers. He dismounted and hitched his unsaddled mount to the post in front of the dispatch office. It was no much of an office, but it was one of the few wooden shanties that had a glass window and fireplace. Lord Carnarvon had the building erected to protect his communications from foreign eyes.

As he traced the front of the dig site dispatch office, Strong recognized the grunt and smell of a camel and followed the sound around the side. In the short time he had been in Egypt, he quickly learned the stench of the camels. Even now, six months later, he had not the courage to mount one, preferring horses in all matters that required a mount. As he rounded the corner into the alleyway, Strong drew his rifle. In that instant, he found himself in the presence of Ms. Stella von Strauss.

She was no less startled than he was, gasping in with a quick, deep breath. Also, she was uncommonly beautiful. Her figure was that of a woman, well-fed but not overly so. Her features—long, wavy blonde hair and bright blue eyes—were so uncommon in this part of the world that she seemed alien to him. When she recognized his face, she smiled, showing off a set of nicely-placed teeth.

"Excuse me, sir," she exalted, letting slip a slight German accent that she had obviously practiced years to stifle. She placed her hand on her chest.

Strong noticed she was wearing khaki pants, a white blouse, and a dark brown jacket. In her attire, she looked ready for an adventure. In fact, Ms. von Strauss was on an adventure, all her own. As acting field correspondent, she was in control of all communication between Lord Carnavon in England and the events at the dig sites. According to Mack, von Strauss had distinguished herself in covert communication during the Great War and was the only blonde woman in a thousand miles. Mack had gone on and on about her the night she arrived. The other men were in awe at her beauty, but often felt trepidation in her presence. Mack, as Dr. Danby's right-hand man, worked with her closely. Strong, however, had only ever seen her a few times. Despite this fact, he could recall every one of her features.

Remembering his duty, Strong attempted to sidestep her and avoid conversation. Von Strauss held up her hand in front of him, index finger pointed upward, like a didactic school teacher.

"What *is* the hurry, Mister..." She parted her lips, pausing for him to fill in his name.

"Strong. Now, please ma'am, step aside. I have business to attend to," he said, pushing himself past her finger. He thought it rude to do so, but he didn't feel like explaining the events that had transpired at the dig site.

As Strong examined the alleyway, he spotted the three camels tied up to a post, their riders nowhere to be seen.

"Your business *is* my business, Mr. Strong," she lessoned him. He wondered if she had been a teacher, or wife, in her life before Egypt. She looked down at his rifle. "What is that rifle for? Is there trouble?"

Dodging her question, Strong inspected the saddlebags on each camel. They were empty. On the building adjacent to the dispatch office, there was a side entrance door. Strong calculated that this was the most likely destination for the thieves, unless they were trying to throw him off their track by leaving the camels here. He didn't figure them for schemers. He remembered von Strauss.

"No, ma'am, but there might be in a second," Strong found the doorknob on the side entrance locked. Strong pushed his shoulder against the door to try and budge it.

Ms. von Strauss began her lecture, "Mr. Strong! I'll have you know that the use of deadly force on locals is highly frowned upon by those in the London office. And…"

The ring from Strong's rifle stopped her banter. He blasted a hole through the lock, but it didn't impress her. In fact, she was fuming. It was apparent that she wasn't ignored often. Strong muscled his way through the door and into the building. Von Strauss followed him.

Immediately, a spray of pistol fire was upon them and Strong dropped to a sitting position behind a large desk. Ms. von Strauss flung herself from the doorway and landed in Strong's lap. For that moment, they locked eyes and he felt her subtle weight pressed down upon him. When a bullet whizzed by their heads, he pushed her off him and onto the floor.

"I know deadly force is frowned upon by those in the London office, but they aren't the ones getting shot at!" Strong yelled, cocking his rifle.

"There must be an army of them!" von Strauss shouted back in response. Her voice could be heard even over the sound of gunfire. Strong found her quite fiery.

The inside of the room was dim, almost dark, but a few lit candles were spread here and there throughout. The dust that had entered through the open doorway made the room hazier. Strong crawled along the side of the desk and saw a gap between the end of the desk and the start of a large table. Between rounds being unloaded in his direction, Strong dove across the gap and found cover beneath the table. There he would bide his time until the attackers were forced to reload.

Back at the desk, Ms. von Strauss was covering her head. She peered from between locks of her golden hair and glanced at Strong. She was obviously frightened, as any woman would be in this situation, but she was not rattled.

To Strong, it seemed, she had been in situations like this before, but was smart enough to know you don't make it out of all of them to be blissfully ignorant of your own mortality. He wished he'd visited the dispatch office more often.

When the gunfire momentarily ceased, Strong popped straight up, aimed his rifle, and fired one shot at the pistoleer across the room. Through the dimly-lit room, Strong didn't expect to hit his mark on the first shot. Despite this, the pistoleer fell like a sack of sand, top heavy from the extra lead in his attic. Strong smirked, pleased with his ability. Rifle still pointed into the haze, Strong canvassed the room with its iron sights. He had counted three thieves back at the dig site, but the other two were nowhere to be seen. He lowered his rifle and noticed the rows of covered tables filling the room. Splayed over the tables and illuminated by the candlelight was the treasure that had been stolen from the dig site.

Strong picked up a small golden figure of an Anubis and inspected it. He wasn't sure if it was from his dig site, but it was definitely genuine. The craftsmanship was exquisite. Ms. von Strauss rose up from behind the desk and assessed the scene in front of her. She slowly walked over to Strong, still unsure if all danger was gone. When she saw the Anubis idol Strong was holding, she grabbed it from his hands. She slowly turned the figure in her hands, rotating it and tilting it to see every inch and crevice. She held it like a jewel long forgotten, but so familiar.

"This—these—are from one of Lord Carnarvon's dig sites," she said, as if talking to herself. "I remember this particular Anubis from a letter I sent him months ago. I thought it had been returned to the dig site for proper storage."

"It is from one of Carnarvon's sites—Danby's," Strong placed his rifle sling over his shoulder and picked up another artifact.

"What—how?" Mumbled von Strauss, obviously not used to being outwitted, as her face had a difficult time twisting into a look of confusion.

Strong explained the events at the dig site to her and left out some of the more gruesome details. He recalled that Mack had two of the looter's henchmen in his care and they were likely to talk when he got hold of them. In place of von Strauss' confusion came a look of irritation.

"Your use of deadly force may be overlooked in the wake of the retrieval of our stolen goods," she explained, placing the Anubis back on the table in his spot.

"Oh, thank God," replied Strong, sarcastically, lowering his rifle.

Ms. von Strauss didn't pick up on his mockery, or simply ignored it.

"Why would they just leave all this loot?" It seemed obvious that she had not intended to ponder aloud, but her genuine curiosity overcame her.

"I'm not sure," replied Strong, "what is this building?"

Von Strauss took a quick glance around her to recall where she was. She began, "Well, it was a foreign embassy at some point. Maybe a year back. Now, however, it stands vacant. I suspect squatters have taken it for their own."

Ms. von Strauss left to send a boy to retrieve diggers to bring men back to properly package and store the stolen artifacts. Alone in the vacant building, Strong thought to himself: Why would three thieves risk life and limb and then leave behind their prize? He hoped the looter henchman that Mack detained would reveal more information.

Once the diggers stored and transported the artifacts, von Strauss accompanied Strong back to the dig site. She wanted to make sure the artifacts found a safe and proper home and to see how Dr. Danby was coming with his agenda. Strong and von Strauss traveled on a newly built wagon pulled by a team of six horses. Strong's unsaddled mount strolled behind it. The hunt for the perfect mummy—and the most gold—was on in Egypt. Ever since the first archeologist had pulled the first disfigured personage from the sand, white men trampled every ancient temple and burial site in Egypt. Lord Carnarvon had poured his family's wealth into Egyptian dig workers, supplies, archeologists' wages, and, yet, had nothing to show for it other than some artifacts and pottery. It had been barely enough to break even.

Upon their arrival to the dig site, they found it in a state of euphoria. Dig workers were drinking bottled spirits and a large crowd was assembled in the center of camp.

"Is this how you all spend your time in camp?" asked von Strauss.

Strong didn't reply, but stepped down from the wagon and walked toward camp. Von Strauss climbed down on her own and followed him. Strong had never seen the camp in such a fervor. The only experience he had with the camp in such excitement was the time a travelling brothel made a stop at the edge of camp. To everyone's dismay, Dr. Danby had the brothel train move down the road away from the site.

Strong was searching for Mack among the crowd of people. Most were Egyptian or Turkish, so a white man, especially one with a bald head like Mack, was relatively easy to find. After a moment, he caught sight of Mack. Strong placed a hand on his shoulder, and Mack turned to look at him. Mack grabbed Strong in a bearhug and squeezed him tight.

"Glad to see me?" Strong asked, jokingly.

"Yes, of course," replied Mack. He was smiling the biggest Strong had seen in ages. Aside, of course, from his days with the traveling brothel.

After a handshake, Strong asked Mack what all the fuss was about. Ms. von Strauss was silent behind them.

Mack's face was lit up with excitement, asking, "Good news or bad news first?"

Strong and von Strauss traveled on wagon pulled by a team of six horses.

Strong playfully punched Mack in the arm and protested, "Just spill it, old boy."

Mack quickly replied, "Bad news is those dogs got free somehow. I found their lashings cut clean and their trail cold. Don't worry, though, we'll find 'em soon enough."

Strong was in shock. He had anticipated questioning those goons the whole ride back to camp. "What's the good news, then?"

Mack yelled with glee, "Carter has found Tut's tomb in the Valley of the Kings!"

The next day, Strong accompanied von Strauss around camp while she saw to the general state of things. Every digger was loathsome to work with after a night full of booze and excitement. After she ensured the successful packaging of the stolen artifacts from the day prior, von Strauss wanted to speak with Dr. Danby and hear more about Carter's find. After all, it would be her job to write to Lord Carnarvon about the glorious event. As they walked in the direction of Dr. Danby's tent, she inquired about the beast Strong held in his hands.

"Haraami," explained Strong, "is my little hunter." The ferret looked up at Strong when he said her name, but didn't move. She was comfortable in his clutches.

"Haraami? Maybe a little thief, I suppose," von Strauss leaned in to touch the ferret, but Haraami hissed and climbed her way into Strong's satchel that hung at his hip.

"Sorry about that, she's feisty. Like all women," he closed the flap on his satchel to protect Haraami from the heat.

"Do you have a woman, Mr. Strong? A Mrs. Strong?" Her question was loaded more than the rifle at his back. He felt himself get red in the face and stumbled to answer.

"Uh, no. Not really, I mean. I've been with a woman, I mean," he replied, unsatisfied with his response. He waited for her smart reply.

"So have I, Mr. Strong," she said. Her comment caught him off guard. "But, my question was: do you *have* a woman?"

He smirked, "No. No, I don't. Never been married, either. After the war, wives are few and far between. The good ones are still married and the bad ones, well, they aren't here, that's for sure."

"That's true, Mr. Strong. Most good women are at home, caring for die Kinder—I mean children," she kicked sand after her mishap. She went silent.

Strong realized her apprehension. It wasn't easy being a German out of

Germany after the Great War. Hell, it was hard being anybody out of anywhere after such a thing. He slowed his pace and said, "Call me Harvey. By the way, it's okay that you're German. I can hear it in your voice. I know a lot about the place, actually."

"Thank you," she looked up at him, hesitantly. "You may call me Stella." She paused, then asked, "Were you stationed there? Saw action, I mean?"

He paused, choosing his words correctly, "No, but I saw action near the German borders. I was injured at the Siege of Antwerp. I learned about Germany from the Belgians."

"What was your injury?" She asked, but quickly made a redaction, "I'm sorry. I should not have asked such a thing."

"No—it's fine. My horse, Houdini, took a slug to the chest and flung me. I had three broken ribs and a torn ligament. It wasn't a real battle injury, but it hurt the same."

"Houdini? After Harry Houdini, the performer?"

"Yes, actually," he smiled.

"I saw him perform when I was a girl, at Scotland Yard. He escaped numerous handcuffs, even when wearing multiple sets. Strange man," she said, throwing back her wavy hair.

"Scotland Yard? Long way from Germany."

"Yes, I know. My father was an archeologist who traveled extensively. He would work anywhere for pay, but his real love was Egypt. He hoped to unearth every mummy in Egypt, he told me once. We were there for business, but he left me with his assistant. She took me to see Houdini."

As von Strauss finished her story, the pair arrived at Dr. Danby's tent. The good doctor was likely inside, laying out plans for further excavation of his site. In the wake of Carter's find, Danby would be under immense pressure to find something of equal or greater value to keep his job.

Before she entered the tent, von Strauss stopped and looked back at Strong. "Harvey?"

Strong turned back toward her, and replied, "Yes?"

"Thank you for speaking with me. It's not often you find someone—especially a man, in these parts—who cares to hear a woman's idle conversation."

"No. I enjoy it, actually. Haraami doesn't talk much."

Ms. von Strauss giggled. She disappeared into the tent. Strong smiled, pleased with himself.

As Harvey Strong shuffled the deck and put in his ante, Mack continued where he had left off before downing a swig of whisky, "Fucking Carter got to outdo us all!"

For the past hour, the men had been speaking about Carter's find. Certain kings and burial sites were common knowledge in Egypt, especially among archeologists and diggers. King Tut, the boy king whose tomb had yet to be discovered, was said to contain immense riches. For the diggers, riches meant gold and silver, money to feed their families. For the Egyptologists and lords in England, riches meant preserved mummies and world renown. For Strong, it meant more work.

"They say Tut's tomb contains treasures beyond reckoning," declared Gideon Belsky, one of Strong's four-man security unit. Belsky had been here longer than Strong, but was passed over for the head-of-security position on account of his Jewish origin.

"Yeah," began Greg Hardin, another one of Strong's men, "I heard Nefertiti's mummy has gilded tits!"

The men argued for some time about Nefertiti's gilded tits, whether mummies had tits, and whether or not Nefertiti was even a real person. Mack stumbled into the conversation with talk of ancient Egyptian weaponry. He was clutching a bottle of his favorite label, Stauer's, a German brand of whisky.

"They say Tut's most prized possession was his personal dagger: a gift of the gods," said Mack, hiccuping.

"Gift from the gods?" Asked Joe Howard, who was not part of Strong's team but was another one of the Englishmen employed by Lord Carnarvon. Strong couldn't recall his job.

"Yes," Mack continued, "they say the heavens brought down a shower of meteors that grew green with supernatural powers. According to legend, the boy king had a dagger made from these rocks."

"Bullshit!" Shouted Joel Killroy, one of Strong's unit, swiping a shot glass from the table. It fell into the sand.

"Hmmm," pondered Joe, scratching his barely-bearded chin, "must be worth a pretty penny."

Marcus Martell, the fourth and final member of Strong's security unit, chimed in, "Quite a few pretty pennies, I'd bet."

"Actually," Mack went on, "the value of the cosmic dagger lay in the cosmic portion. Along with glowing green when wielded, they say the dagger could penetrate any armor or shield. Apparently, Tut kept it on him at all times."

Strong sat silent, not paying attention to much of what the men said. He was probably the most sober of the bunch. He was still analyzing the day's events. He didn't care much about Carter's find. Sure, mummies and daggers were nice, but he had felt bested by the looter henchmen who had escaped and was in a somber mood. He was angry with Mack for letting them slip away. He pondered why they had left behind their loot.

As Mack threw down his cards and revealed five aces, the other men threw their cards at him and called him a cheat. Strong laughed at Mack's facial expressions, but his mind wandered to Ms. von Strauss. He remembered her blue eyes, her voluptuous figure, and the smell of her hair. He thought of leaving the tent and searching her out in the village.

Just then, a digger burst through the tent doors.

"Sirs! I just came from the village. A terrible thing has happened!" said thhe boy, who was no more than sixteen. He was out of breath from running. The men around the card table sat quiet.

"Well, spill it," commanded Belsky.

"Ms. von Strauss has been taken—kidnapped!"

The group looked around at each in astonishment. Sure, women were kidnapped fairly often in these parts. The poorer women were treated like slaves and property. However, the kidnapping of a prominent white women would echo throughout the villages. Mack jumped to his feet, wobbled and fell back in his chair.

Strong clenched his fists, thinking of von Strauss. He could feel his body heating up with anger. While he had no evidence to substantiate it, he knew the looters and their henchmen were responsible for her kidnapping. He thought of her chained up, beat up, possibly raped. His mind was made up as the words spilled from the boy messenger's mouth: he was going after her.

The next morning, Strong, Mack, and the team packed their horses and galloped off in the direction of the village where von Strauss was last seen. Strong had laid out the plan to his men before they left: pack guns and water, question everything we hear and see, and look for a white woman with blonde hair. Other than Strong and Mack, none of the men had seen Ms. von Strauss in person. Luckily, they all respected Strong and were happy enough to get to ride somewhere and possibly shoot their guns. Haraami rode in Strong's left saddlebag, careful not to stick her nose out too far to avoid the whirling sands. When they arrived in the village, Strong began with the dispatch office where von Strauss worked. Mack accompanied him inside while the other four men spread out to question people. Once inside the dispatch office, Strong questioned the nervous clerk at the desk.

"And did she say where she was going when she left?"

"No—but I assumed bed."

Strong slammed his first down on the desk, "Oh really—bed? How might you know the location of her bed?"

"No, not that way," said the clerk, sweating, "she looked tired and it was late; I just assumed."

"Did Ms. von Strauss speak to anyone after she returned to the office yesterday?"

The clerk thought for a moment. He began to speak, but stopped himself.

Strong slammed his first on the desk again and shouted, "Well?"

"Yes! Yes, she did. Mr. Erich von Radetz, a Behomian proprietor who has an office down the way. Ms. von Strauss and Mr. von Radetz speak often." The clerk wiped his brow with his handkerchief.

Strong lifted his fist from the desk, "Thank you, sir."

He turned and left the office. Once outside, Strong rounded up the team and they marched to the office of Erich von Radetz. His office was eight doors (tents included) down on the left and above the door to his wooden shanty hung a sign: "Von Radetz Enterprises. No Vagrants." As Greg Hardin began to knock on the door, Strong muscled past him and kicked in the door. It busted from its hinges and drooped over like a bell-rung boxer.

"After you, sir," said Hardin, sarcastically.

Strong didn't notice the comment. He walked into the office, looked around, up and down, and sighed. It was empty. A lonely desk sat in the corner with some papers scattered on top. There was a separated room and, upon further inspection, was found to be von Radetz's sleeping quarters. Strong began rummaging through the papers on the desk. Mack sensed anger bubbling inside Strong.

"She's probably with those dogs who escaped yesterday. They're probably looking for a ransom. She'll be fine." He placed a hand on Strong's back.

Strong swiftly turned to face him. "If they wanted cash they would've taken that loot. I told yah—it was all left behind, like what they really wanted wasn't there."

Mack had no response. To him, the trail seemed cold.

Strong continued. "She's just part of the puzzle. They—whoever they are—could've taken her months ago. They're after something else—something more valuable."

Mack rolled the lit cigarette between his lips and thought to himself. The other men walked around the office, inspecting everything. On von Radetz's desk, Strong picked up a letter with a note written in German. Strong motioned to Belsky, who was an Austrian Jew. He could speak and read German. Strong handed Belsky the letter.

"*Karte befindet*—Map located. *Treffen Sie sich an Carter das Grab von morgen*—Meet at Carter's tomb tomorrow. *Bringen Sie Hämmer*—Bring hammers," related Belsky, handing the letter back to Strong.

Something more valuable, thought Strong. He turned to Mack. "Where is the most valuable place in Egypt, as we speak?"

Mack pondered for a second, then replied, "The Valley of the Kings; Tut's tomb."

Mack was exactly right. Carter's discovery of Tut's burial tomb was going to bring every correspondent and vulture in Egypt looking to plunder stories and artifacts. Whoever had Ms. von Strauss—if money was their purpose—was going to Carter's dig site. *To do what?* Strong wasn't sure. Steal Tut's mummy, pilfer artifacts, ransom the girl; there were endless possibilities. With that in mind, and now von Radetz' note to back it up, Strong had a solid lead. He pocketed the note and the group headed east into the Valley of the Kings.

At Carter's dig site, a crowd was gathered to witness history. Diggers slowly moved stone and sand; Englishmen huddled in groups speculating what they would find, and even a group of three gentlemen traveled from France to witness the opening. To everyone's dismay, the opening was not going to happen any time soon.

With Ms. von Strauss missing, Carter had written Lord Carnarvon himself about his epic find. Naturally, the English lord decided it was best to see the site in person. It would be two, maybe three weeks before the seal was broken, the mud-plastered doorway pried open, and Tut's treasures explored. All this according to a local boy—six, maybe seven years old—who was selling information for coin.

"Thanks," said Strong in Egyptian Arabic, throwing the boy a small copper coin. He turned to Mack, "Well, everybody's here who matters or wants to matter. It seems everyone has forgotten a white woman has been kidnapped. Either way, there's gotta be somebody here who knows or has seen our looters."

"I don't know, Boss, but we have a shadow."

Mack pointed out a man standing ten feet behind them. He was staring toward the crowd, but it was obvious that the corners of his eyes watched them. He wore a turban and a Mauser C96 tucked into his sash.

"How many locals do you know who own a Mauser?" Strong asked Mack, who inspected the pistol at the man's hip.

"None," Mack replied.

It was likely that this man had been given this pistol. Strong thought: Mr. von Radetz, perhaps? After all, he was Bohemian and would have access to German weaponry. Now that Strong thought about it, the looter henchman who attacked him while riding a camel was using a Mauser C96. Could von Radetz have a crew of these cronies working for him? It is possible that Ms. von Strauss got caught up in the hustle and was taken as collateral damage. Not if Harvey Strong could help it.

Strong motioned to Mack, who slipped back into the crowd to circle back and tail their shadow. To distract their shadow, Strong walked away from the dig site and chose a long row of tents down which to take a stroll. He petted Haraami on his shoulder as he walked.

The shadow followed, casually tracking Strong's movements down the row of tents. Along the way, a few diggers exited their sleeping quarters and passed them. Soon, Strong and this shadow passed beyond earshot of the dig site and found themselves alone amidst the forest of tents and sea of sand.

All the while, Strong tried not to look behind him at his shadow to avoid giving away his knowledge, but the man was close enough now that Strong could see the glimmer of a blade out of the corner of his eye. Fearing a blindside attack, Strong turned swiftly and saw the man raise a large knife overhead and prepare to stab him. Before the blade found its mark, Mack appeared from behind a tent and tackled the man to the ground. Strong kicked the blade from the man's hands and Mack wrestled him into a nearby tent. The commotion scared Haraami and she scurried away from the scene.

Inside the tent, which was fortunately empty of watchful eyes, Strong forcibly removed the man's turban to get a better look at his face. He was shocked to see the brand of a cobra burned into the man's forehead. The brand was healed over and looked to be done with some care. Mack grabbed the man's head and lit into him with his right first. The man spit blood and said a curse in Arabic. Strong reached down, pulled his knife from its hip sheath, and pointed the end into the man's throat.

"Speak English?" Asked Strong. The words seemed to glide over the man's face like a mist.

Strong shoved the blade deeper into the man's neck, piercing his skin and asked, "Speak English now?"

The man spit blood in Strong's face. Mack wrestled him into the sand. As Strong wiped his face with a white handkerchief, Haraami appeared from beneath the tent's canvas covering and ran to him. He placed her on his shoulder. Mack was choking the man, so Strong called him off, at least momentarily.

"Talk or you're gettin' more of my friend here," said Strong, pointing to Mack. The man stared blankly at them, but when Strong motioned for Mack to have at him, the man pleaded for mercy.

"Okay, okay! I talk," shouted the man.

He petted Haraami on his shoulder...

Strong knelt down beside him and asked, "Why are you following us?"

"Orders. Must follow," he said, in broken English.

"Orders? Who's your boss—your leader... *zaeim*?"

The man spit another glob of blood on the ground, then said, "Leader is *Alkubra*." His eyes gleamed with pride and fear, but not in his current captors.

Mack replied, "*Alkubra* means cobra in Arabic. I've heard the diggers shouting it at night when they find an unwanted guest in the sleeping quarters. Maybe it's von Radetz's pseudonym."

Strong grabbed the man's cotton robes and asked, "Where is Alkubra? Does he have von Strauss? White—*abyad*—woman—*nisa*?"

The man smiled with his bloody set of teeth, "Yes—*abyad nisa*—very pretty."

Strong walloped the man in his jaw and shouted, "Where is she?"

"Inside," said the man, blood gurgling in his throat.

"Inside where?" Asked Mack, who knelt down beside the man.

The man's eyes went squirrely and he seemed to wobble, disoriented.

Strong shook him, shouting, "Inside where? Village—town—tent?"

The man gurgled again, letting out a sigh and whispered, "Tomb."

Inspecting the man's body, Strong found a small dart sticking out his thigh. The man had poisoned himself.

"Why'd he do that?" Asked Mack.

"He didn't want to be captured, I suppose," Strong guessed.

"He already was," said Mack, lifting to his feet, "by us."

Strong did the same and replied, "Not by us—by his boss, Alkubra."

The man's body was limp and the cobra brand on his forehead mocked Strong.

"I don't know why Alkubra has von Strauss, but now we know where to go," said Strong, sheathing his knife.

Mack prodded him with a glance.

"Inside—he said—tomb; Must mean inside the Tut's tomb,' Strong turned his head toward the dig site.

"The tomb? It hasn't even been opened yet."

"I don't know how, either. We'll have to investigate further."

With the newfound knowledge of Ms. von Strauss' captor, Alkubra, Strong and Mack reconvened with the security team at the tent. Belsky and Killroy were sent to ask the diggers for any information about a white woman, while Hardin and Martell were sent into the crowd to look for von Radetz. To avoid detection, at no point were they to speak the name Alkubra.

As for Strong and Mack, they would seek counsel with the local wali, or helper. For the Egyptians, these men were like holy men, but more so custodians of legend and prophecy. They hoped he would have information about the mysterious Alkubra.

A group of young boys agreed to take them to the wali for a nickel each, and escorted them to a run-down tent at the edge of camp. The wali sometimes traveled extensively, seeing all and knowing all. Most people didn't believe in their powers, but respected them as tradition. Strong didn't believe anything except what the eyes saw. And for now, a wali must do.

Inside the tent, which was covered in relics and rugs from around the country, sat a small, old man covered in red robes. The wali sat cross-legged in the center of the tent, lighting an incense candle. He had a scraggly beard of white hair. He summoned them inside and they sat in front of him.

"You seek knowledge, not help," clarified the wali. His English was the best Strong had heard among natives.

"Yes," Strong confirmed.

"The knowledge you seek is ancient and should not be spoken plainly," warned the wali.

Strong noticed that nothing he said was very specific, but could really be applied to any knowledge that someone would seek a wali for help finding. He doubted the old man's true identity.

"Yes," Strong agreed.

"Ask your question. I feel it burn within you." The wali didn't look at the men in their faces, but worked with an incense candle at his feet.

"We seek information about Alkubra," queried Strong.

The wali immediately stopped fiddling with the candle, placed it onto the plate, and looked up at Strong. The wali ran his fingers across his own forehead and then made the motion of a cobra striking.

"Alkubra… a name I have not heard in ages. Not many speak of this anymore."

"What can you tell us?" Asked Mack.

"Alkubra is both a name and an order. In ancient times, when the pharaohs ruled and the pyramids stood tall, Alkubra was the seeker. Alkubra sought the *slah min alssamawat.*"

"What does that mean?" Strong leaned closer to the wali.

"*Slah min alssamawat* means dagger from the heavens. A weapon more powerful than any the world has seen. The pharaoh wielded this weapon, toppling cities and keeping peace. The *eshr awlia al'umur*—Ten Guardians—protected it after his death, until his heir was strong enough to wield it, too."

"So how does Alkubra factor in?" Mack inquired.

"Alkubra—the cobra—sought to control the dagger. He, and his order, would stop at nothing to take it for themselves."

Strong spoke next. "Do the Guardians or the Alkubra still exist?"

The wali leaned in forward and replied, "Do you sit in my tent?"

Harvey Strong struggled for sleep. The silence in camp allowed his mind to wander through the fights with Alkubra's men, his talks with von Strauss, and his new knowledge on this ancient war for the cosmic dagger. It all seemed like something out of a dime novel or a story he would have dreamt up as a kid. After an hour of tossing and turning in his cot, he rose out of bed, content with being awake. He grabbed his boots and checked for scorpions. Then, quiet as a church-mouse, he snuck out of the tent to avoid waking the group. Haraami looked up from her spot on the cot, but Strong didn't motion for her to follow.

Throwing his rifle sling onto his shoulder, Strong began walking to clear his head. At night, the dig site was dead quiet. No carts were being pulled full of stone and sand, the men were all asleep in their cots, and the creatures were silent as the grave. The blue of the Egyptian moon seemed to permeate every crevice of sand that Strong passed. His own shadow followed him as he traversed the narrow rows of tents. He passed the tents of the French gentlemen, Howard Carter's tent, piles of displaced stone and sand, and finally arrived at the entrance to Tut's tomb. Sealing the doors shut was one piece of strong rope, likely blessed, or cursed, to protect its contents. After hearing the words of the wali, Strong shuddered at the thought of blessings and curses alike.

Strong inspected the area around the tomb, looking for anything that might allow someone to enter unnoticed, as Alkubra had supposedly done. He didn't notice anything unusual, so he kept walking past the end of the camp and up the side of a large sand dune. As he climbed the dune, he noticed fresh horse tracks in the sand. At the top of the dune, he could almost smell their potent odor in the air. Strong realized the freshness of the tracks and stench. As he reached the precipice of the dune, he fell to his stomach. Strong peered over the edge and saw nearly a dozen horses tied up in a circle, with one man guarding the reins in case they got spooked. The man wore a turban and a kilij at his side. Strong assumed he was one of von Radetz's men—Alkubra's men—immediately.

About ten yards past the horses, a group of five similarly-dressed men spoke in a group. They seemed to be waiting for something, as some smoked and others spit. The largest of the men was sitting on the sand, sharpening his blade. Near his feet, a yawning hole opened up in the sand. Strong noticed the hole had solid edges and he immediately suspected an ancient staircase entrance. With the placement of this entrance, it could potentially be the "back door" of Tut's tomb. Strong suspected the other half dozen men—if his calculations of the amount of horses needed to carry men were correct—were already inside, likely led by Alkubra himself and Ms. von Strauss, his prisoner, in tow. They were searching for the cosmic dagger. What did Ms. von Strauss have to do with it? He wasn't sure.

With no time to waste, he decided against waking Mack and the group. He shuffled his body over the edge and slid down to the horses. He snuck past the handler and crouched behind the nearest horse. Strong removed his rifle and, when he was close enough to hear the man whistling a tune, threw his weight behind the wood stock and drove it into the man's head. He fell easily; out cold.

Fearing detection, Strong dragged the man up the dune and threw him over to the other side. Before going back at the horses, he checked the man's head. Sure enough, emblazoned on his forehead, was the cobra brand. He thought over his options: He could surprise the men and take them out with his rifle. In that event, they might fan out and the shots would wake Carter's whole camp. To ensure Ms. von Strauss' safe return and the capture of Alkubra, Strong knew he must maintain the element of surprise.

With those stakes in mind, he untied the reins of the horses and slapped the flank of the most anxious one. The horses fled, trampling sand in a violent manner. Naturally, this aroused the surprise of the five henchmen. Four took off after their mounts, while one, the savviest of the bunch and the sharpener of swords, stayed behind to inspect why they were spooked.

The henchman walked toward the horses and, squinting his eyes, spotted Strong's silhouette in the moonlight. Strong noticed how big the man was— likely over six and a half feet tall with a large, black beard. The henchman sheathed his sword and pulled his rifle out. Against his better judgment, Strong rushed and swung his rifle at the man's head. The henchman ducked and Strong's rifle went flying into the darkness. The henchman raised his rifle at Strong, who grabbed the barrel and pulled it toward him and to the side of himself.

The momentum propelled the henchman forward and his barrel stuck into the ground. Strong grabbed him from behind by the waist and then put his right hand on the rifle to steal it away. In the struggle, the gun fired, but the sand muffled the sound. The henchman elbowed Strong in the face, but Strong pulled himself through the pain and threw him backward, end over end.

With the rifle gone, Strong pulled his knife. The henchman did the same, but his was a freshly-sharpened kilij. The two circled each other like hungry dogs. The only thing they could make out of each another was the glimmer of white in their eyes and the glint of steel in their blades, as reflected in the moonlight. The henchman made the first move, swinging overhead—a mistake—as Strong capitalized, stabbing the man in the stomach.

The henchmen didn't fall, but writhed in pain and grabbed at his wound. Now, he was angry. He rushed Strong, swinging his kilij again, slicing Strong's forearm. Strong fell back to his rear, but was forced to roll away from an oncoming swoosh of the kilij. The henchman was bleeding from his wound, but kept fighting. Strong jumped to his feet and swung his knife at the henchman. This brought Strong too close to the man, who grabbed him. He lifted Strong above his head and onto his shoulder, squeezing the life from him.

Strong began bashing the man's head with his own, but it only hurt Strong. The henchman dropped his kilij in order to squeeze Strong more tightly. Strong felt the blood rush to his head and a grayness cover his eyes. He knew this was his last chance. He barred his teeth and bit down on the man's nose, tasting blood. The man held on as long as he could, but the pain forced him to drop Strong to the sand.

The henchman, in a mixture of anger and pain, rushed at Strong, who was lying on the sand. Strong noticed the twinkle of steel on the ground, grabbed the henchman's kilij, and stabbed his rushing antagonist in the stomach. The force of henchman's blitz forced him further onto his own blade and his weight pressed his limp body all the way to the hilt.

After a moment, Strong threw the man's limp body off of him and rolled to the side. He took out his handkerchief and wrapped it around his arm where he was cut. He retrieved his knife and wiped the blood off on the henchman's turban. Fishing around for his rifle, Strong stumbled across the henchman's Lee-Enfield MKIII. He checked the stripper clip and was thankful to find all five rounds unfired and clear of sand. Fearing the return of the other henchmen who had taken off after the horses, Strong ran toward the tomb entrance in the sand and plunged himself into the abyss.

Inside the tomb, it was pitch black and the air was thick with ancient dust. As he had suspected, there was a staircase that led to a lower corridor. Strong pulled a matchbook from his front shirt pocket and lit one. He wished he had brought a torch. In the faint flicker of his lone match, he could make out the stone walls—old, but uninteresting—and the beginning of a long passageway.

It seemed to be level, moving slightly downward. Strong looked down and began searching the floor. After a moment, he found some dusty wrappings on the floor and tied them around his knife blade. From his leather satchel, he pulled a bottle of gun oil and poured some on the wrappings. Then, using another match, he lit the makeshift torch.

For nearly thirty yards he walked the empty passageway. As he walked, he thought he could hear something in the passageway with him. He would stop, only to hear nothing. Finally, after assuring himself that he *did* hear something, he turned quickly and threw the torch behind him, pulling his rifle at the same time. The light illuminated Haraami, who jumped backward in terror at the flying torch. She hopped around the torch and ran to Strong. He picked her up.

"What are you doing in here? You should be in the tent, you pest."

There was no time to take her back and she would be lost forever in these tunnels if he left her alone. Haraami made a squeak and he placed her on his shoulder. At the end of the passageway was a wall. He used his torch to look around, but there were no doorways or entrances. Suddenly, his torch flickered. Strong looked down, but saw nothing. Then, he looked up and saw a large hole in the ceiling and a rope hanging down. Strong carefully chucked his torch up into the crevice so that it illuminated the next level. He jumped up and clutched the rope. Haraami held onto his shirt for dear life. Strong easily climbed the rope and was in the second-level within a moment.

From the darkness sprang a henchman, kilij in hand, and caught Strong off-guard. The blade made a swoop at Strong's head, just barely missing, and he fell backward. The momentum of the fall threw Haraami across the passageway. Strong rolled away and pulled the rifle from his back. He knew he could not fire the gun and give away his location, but he would use the rifle to protect himself from the next blow. The kilij struck the barrel and sparks flew in the darkness. On the floor, the torch illuminated the outlines of the men's fighting figures. By their shadows, they might have been mistaken for dancers. The henchman made another swing at Strong, who used the rifle to block the blow and sent the henchman falling face-first to the floor.

As the henchman searched for his kilij that had disappeared into the darkness, Strong picked up his torch from the floor, rushed the man, and stabbed him with the flaming blade directly in the chest. Strong pulled the extinguished blade from the henchman's chest. The man made a low, squealing sound, wobbled backward, and fell down through the hole in the floor. Strong lit a match to set fire to his torch again and then dropped the match into hole. It stayed lit long enough to reveal the henchman's lifeless body at the bottom.

After grabbing Haraami from the corner she was hiding in, Strong continued down the second-level, rounded a corner and saw a large hole broken through the wall. The passageway continued down, but the hole interested Strong. It would have taken at least three men using hammers to bust through the wall. Strong remembered the note from von Radetz' office: "Bringen Sie Hämmer."

"Bring hammers," uttered Strong, remembering Belsky's translation.

Realizing this must be the work of von Radetz's—Alkubra's—henchmen, Strong inspected the new doorway more intricately. Above the hole, the figure of a scarab beetle with falcon's wings was carved into the stone wall. Strong knew the scarab figured extensively into Egyptian culture, but was unsure what it represented exactly. He thought he would find out soon enough, so he crawled through the hole.

Inside was a large room with stone walls that was supported by four stone pillars in each corner. In front of him was a staircase leading downward and, below, the room was illuminated. He was on the balcony and from here he could get a good look at the scene below. Strong realized his torch might be visible, so he extinguished it and re-sheathed his knife. Strong crept closer to the edge of the balcony and peered over the wall.

In the room below lay ten sarcophagi, each with the same scarab beetle figure carved on top. Immediately, Strong remembered the words of the wali: the Ten Guardians! The Ten Guardians protected the cosmic dagger upon the pharaoh's death. These must be the tombs of those Ten Guardians. The scarab beetle must be their insignia, like the cobra is for the Alkubra, thought Strong. Then, he noticed the remaining three henchmen, who were using hammers to bust open the tops of each sarcophagus and then rummaging through the insides. Mummies, as well as artifacts, were strewn about the room like they meant nothing. Knowing the time for action was afoot, Strong raised his rifle and set it on the balcony wall. Just as his finger touched the trigger, the barrel of a pistol touched the back of his head.

Harvey Strong was between a rock and hard place: The hard steel of the pistol pushed against the back of his head pressed him flat against the stone balcony wall. The henchman holding the pistol to his head shouted something in Arabic to someone below. A voice cackled back in response and Strong was pushed toward the staircase. The voice that called out orders was not one Strong expected. It was not the voice of a Bohemian man named von Radetz. It didn't have the characteristics of a Bohemian accent nor the characteristics of a man. It was the voice of a woman—with the hint of a German accent.

Strong was led down the staircase and passed the sarcophagi that were being destroyed by the other henchmen. Strong had miscounted the number of henchmen. He counted twelve horses outside. Four henchmen had chased after them, he had dealt with three, and that left five horses. He figured three for the henchmen, one for Ms. von Strauss, and one for the villain he had long been chasing: Alkubra.

Only, it seemed to Strong—as he was thrown in front of a person wearing white satin robes and a large golden figure of cobra on her head of blonde hair—that he had overestimated his intelligence and underestimated the savvy of a young woman.

Ms. von Strauss, whom he had figured for a damsel in distress, was Alkubra. The golden cobra coiled up on her headpiece was evidence of that, as well as the henchmen that so quickly abided her orders. She stared down at Strong as if from a throne. She was still beautiful, but her eyes held long-hidden menace.

"What—why?" Strong managed to say, perplexed.

"Don't fret, Mr. Strong," she said with an air of power, "remember: your business is my business."

The sound of a hammer breaking through a sarcophagus woke Strong from his disbelief.

"You—all along? The looters, the 'kidnapping', the shadows that followed me," Strong said, still piecing together the events of the past week, "but why?" To what end?"

Von Strauss laughed in pleasant surprise. The golden cobra curled on her head like a crown wiggled with her laugh. Despite the confusion that she was currently causing him, he still admired her face. He remembered how they walked together and spoke of home. He wished to return to that time. Everything was so simple then.

"Harvey, don't you understand? There is a prize here—more powerful and expensive than any mummy that Carter could pull out of the sand," said von Strauss.

"The dagger," said Strong, with realization.

Behind him, the henchmen were opening the last two sarcophagi.

"Yes," she said, "The cosmic dagger is the ultimate prize in Egypt. Most do not believe in its power, but I know otherwise. My father, as I told you, was an egyptologist. On Ted Davis' dig in 1907, they found this hidden corridor and within, they found the dagger. When wielded, it glows green and makes the wielder invincible."

Strong was amazed. All along, he had been fighting a war he didn't know existed.

He mustered the courage to inquire, "If your father found it—why don't

Ms. von Strauss...was Alkubra.

you have it?"

"This room holds the remains of the original ten *eshr awlia al'umur*—the Ten Guardians. They stole the dagger from my father and hid it here. Only recently did I finally figure out the exact location," said von Strauss, pacing around the room.

"You are Alkubra," Strong grabbed Haraami from his shoulder and put her on the ground. She scampered off to a hiding place.

"Right you are, Harvey. My, you are smarter than you look. I knew you were different from the moment we met."

With a final boom, the tenth and final sarcophagus was opened. From inside, the henchmen pulled two items wrapped in dusty cloth. The first was a glass scarab necklace, with the same feathered wings as the symbol on the tomb's entrance. The other wrap revealed a golden sheath and knife handle. One henchman, who bore the cobra brand on his forehead, knelt and presented the blade to von Strauss. She smiled as she held the dagger.

"My father was *Alkubra* and, when he died, I took his title," she ranted. "It is—was—my mission to find the cosmic dagger and restore order to the world. Unfortunately, the Ten Guardians were not gone after all. Erich von Radetz, a Bohemian entrepreneur and the last guardian, was the last thing standing in my way. With him gone, and the map in my possession, finding the cosmic dagger was only too simple."

In one swift motion, von Strauss pulled the dagger from its sheath and the meteorite blade glowed green. She smiled, revealing her familiar white teeth. Strong lowered his head in disappointment. She re-sheathed the dagger and put it in her sash. She grabbed the scarab necklace from her follower and placed it around Strong's neck.

Strong lifted his head and asked, "What's this for?"

She smirked, "A gift—for keeping people distracted with that kidnapping nonsense—and for rescuing me."

She slowly kissed him on the lips. At that moment, a shot rang out in the hollow room. The henchman behind Strong fell to the floor dead, a hole through his head. Strong turned and saw Mack and the crew at the top of the staircase, guns blazing.

The other henchman took cover behind the sarcophagi, but von Strauss didn't. She stepped past Strong and pulled the dagger from her sash. She threw the dagger with such force that is passed through the chest of Marcus Martell and was lodged into the wall behind him. Martell wavered and fell dead. Before the men could fire again, the dagger was dislodged from the wall by some invisible force and returned to von Strauss' hand like a boomerang.

Seeing her power, Mack and the others dove for cover. As Strong stood up, the glass scarab beetle around his neck glowed green. Strong grabbed the dead henchman's pistol and began firing at the others.

Dagger back in hand, von Strauss threw it again, this time sending it through Joel Killroy's neck. He, too, fell dead. Mack leaned his head from around the pillar to assess the situation. With immense force, von Strauss threw the dagger. It broke through the two-foot thick stone pillar and lodged itself in Mack's shoulder. He cried out in pain.

The roof began to tremble from the loss of the support pillar. Everyone's gaze went upward as rock fell from the ceiling. Mack collapsed to the floor as the dagger was ripped from his flesh and returned to von Strauss. Seeing the attempted assassination of his best friend infuriated Strong. He raised his pistol, pointed it at von Strauss, and cocked back the hammer. She turned to face him and smiled.

"Harvey, you can't stop me," she said. "Join me. Don't you want to be there when I overtake Egypt? England? Hell—the world?!"

She was drunk with power. In her psychotic rage she threw the dagger and disarmed Strong with ease. He clutched his bleeding hand.

"No, I don't want to be there," shouted Strong over the rumble of the collapsing ceiling. "This world isn't perfect, but it works just fine for me. That dagger will only lead to your destruction, Stella. Please, stop this now, while you still can."

With his final word, von Strauss seemed to come back to reality. She lowered the dagger and looked him in the eyes. For a moment, he had hope for the future—their future. He imagined them together, travelling the world.

"I'm sorry, Harvey," she threw the dagger at his chest.

The force of her throw drove him backward and he fell onto his back. He grabbed for his chest, expecting a dagger to be sticking out of his sternum. Instead, he found the dagger lodged in the thorax of the scarab beetle necklace around his neck.

Seeing her miscalculation, von Strauss extended her hand to beckon the dagger back to her, but the scarab beetle necklace held the dagger in its thorax. The dagger's pull to return to von Strauss lifted the necklace off Strong's chest, but the necklace was strong and didn't break its hold. Another large piece of stone fell from the ceiling, crushing one of the henchmen. At the top of the staircase, Belsky and Hardin helped Mack to his feet and began to head out the corridor.

Mack shouted, "C'mon Harvey! Hurry!"

Strong lifted himself up as von Strauss walked toward him.   She tried to strike him, but without the dagger her power was gone. Strong grabbed her hand to avoid the blow, pulling her in close.

"It's over, Stella" he said. He didn't know whether to kiss her or hit her.

"No, it's not!" She replied with ferocity.

She kneed him in the groin and pulled the necklace from his neck. Her prize in hand, she disappeared through a side exit that Strong had not seen before.

Just then, the upper level dropped out and the staircase, his escape route, was crushed. With no other option, Strong lifted himself up and hobbled after von Strauss. Haraami ran after him, jumping out and clutching onto his pant leg just as the entire room collapsed behind them and darkness reclaimed the tomb of the Ten Guardians.

As the dust settled around him, Strong began to navigate through the room with his hands. He pulled another match from his pocket and lit it. Haraami shrunk back in fear, clinging to Strong's shoulder. The statuesque figure of an Anubis startled him. Behind that, a large golden canopic shrine stood silent. He wondered where they were.

To his left was a doorway and green glow from the adjacent room. He figured this was the dagger and necklace. Strong stepped inside and was amazed at what he saw. Around him, all four walls were painted with gilded figures of people and animals. In the center of the room lay a lone sarcophagus. It was made of solid gold and on top was a solid gold funerary mask. They were in King Tut's burial chamber.

On the other side of the sarcophagus was von Strauss. Her hands were raised and she was wearing the scarab necklace around her neck. The cosmic dagger was still stuck to it. The dagger and scarab were glowing a bright green.

"Even trapped in this amulet, the dagger's power is still strong. Just by wearing this necklace, I have the strength of a dozen men," said von Strauss.

She grabbed the edges of the granite lid and lifted it up with ease, dropping it to the side of the sarcophagus. It would've taken a dozen men to accomplish this feat. With Tut's mummy in sight, Strong knew it was the time to act. In one swift motion, he rushed von Strauss and tackled her to the ground. He ripped the necklace away and threw it across the burial chamber.

When von Strauss lifted herself up, she threw her golden cobra headpiece and chanted an incantation as it dropped to the sand. The golden cobra sprang to life, hissing and snapping at Strong. Strong retreated from the cobra's strikes, never letting it out of his sight. He kicked sand at it, but it kept coming. As Strong tried to kick sand at it again, he tripped over a large canopic jar and fell to the ground. As the cobra readied to strike, Haraami leapt from the darkness and tackled the cobra. The snake leapt at Haraami, but the ferret was too quick to be bitten. They engaged in a battle to the death.

With the cobra distracted, Strong turned his attention back to von Strauss, who had rushed to find the necklace in the darkness. She was wearing the necklace and walking toward him. He tried to rush her, but she pushed him backward five feet and against the stone wall. Strong grabbed a golden plate and threw it at her, but she raised her arm and shattered the plate in mid-air.

In the sand, Haraami dodged a bite by the cobra, leapt its tail, and bit into the cobra's neck. The bite was just high enough to keep the cobra from biting. Seeing her pet in distress, von Strauss grabbed a golden cup and threw it at Haraami. The cup hit her in the side and the ferret was thrown into the sand. Haraami struggled to get back to her feet.

With von Strauss distracted, Strong rushed her. He managed to catch her off-guard and they fell to the ground. He pried the necklace off her and tried to pull the dagger free, but it wouldn't budge. Behind him, the cobra sprang and lodged its fangs in Strong's neck. He felt a burning sensation on his neck and two spots of blood began trickling down to his chest. As Strong felt he cobra's venom run through his veins, the cobra coiled back up and returned to its gilded form. Strong fell to his knees and his blood dripped onto the scarab beetle. The dagger was dislodged and fell into his hands. He fell backward into the sand.

Seeing her opportunity, von Strauss grabbed the dagger from his hands and raised it to eye level. She smiled and saw her reflection in the green glow of the blade. She felt her power restored, ready to rule the world.

As Strong lay in the sand, his blood permeated the scarab beetle on his necklace. Slowly, the beetle wiggled to life and dislodged itself from the necklace. It crawled to von Strauss and up her back. In the chaos of trying to swipe the beetle off her back, she dropped the dagger into the sand. The beetle crawled around her neck, into her mouth, and then devoured her from the inside out. Her white satin robes fell empty to the sandy floor.

Feeling faint, Strong crawled toward the dagger. With his last ounce of effort, he clutched the dagger's handle and its power rejuvenated him. As the cosmic dagger's ancient force worked through him, he felt a rush of power run through his body. He grabbed at his neck, but the cobra's bite marks slowly closed up and were gone. Only dried blood remained on his neck and chest.

As he lifted himself up from the sand, the scarab beetle crawled out of von Strauss' empty robes and started toward Strong. He was nervous that the beetle would devour him, too, but the dagger's power made him feel invincible. Instead of devouring him, the beetle crawled back into the necklace and hardened to its glassy form.

At that moment, Strong realized what an unstoppable force he could be with the cosmic dagger and scarab beetle necklace. One acted as a weapon, the other as a shield. Strong suspected that the dagger was the possession of the pharaoh and the scarab beetle necklace belonged to the Ten Guardians; an ancient system of checks and balances. As the thought of immense power ran through his mind, Strong caught sight of von Strauss' empty robes. This, he thought, is the price you must pay for power. She was gone, and he wanted no part of that.

Strong lifted himself to his feet and walked to King Tut's sarcophagus. Inside the gilded coffin lay the small, frail mummy of a boy king. Strong placed the dagger on Tut's thigh and, with the remaining power of the necklace, was able to lift the granite lid of the sarcophagus back in place.

Strong put the necklace under his shirt for safe keeping and sought out Haraami's body in the sand. He felt her limp body. Luckily, nothing appeared to be broken.

"My little protector," whispered Strong.

Rest would fix her injuries. He placed her in the crook of his arm and looked around. As he leaned against the sealed sarcophagus, the Egyptian hieroglyphics carved on the walls stared back at him. He could not read them—never could—but now he felt as if he could understand them.

Had it not been for the millennia of ancient bugs eating a man-sized hole in the ceiling above the golden canopic shrine, Harvey Strong would have become a mummy, too. As he wriggled through the crawlspace, careful not to hurt Haraami in his satchel, he thought of Carter and Lord Carnarvon finding the dead bodies of an American and his pet ferret. He laughed at the idea.

Once back on the surface, the Egyptian sun forced him to cover his eyes; He had been in the darkness too long. He left friends down there; men and women whom no one would remember. That was now his burden—he must be their memorial. He must live for them.

Strong stumbled his way toward the tent of the wasi. Once inside, he sat down in front of the old man, who was lighting an incense candle. Strong pulled a bundle of white satin robes from his satchel. Pulling away the fabric, he revealed a gilded scarab necklace. Then, he presented them to the wasi, who reached out and took it.

"These are for the *eshr awlia al'umur*—the Ten Guardians," said Strong.

Haraami peeked her head out from around Strong's neck.

"Do the Ten Guardians truly exist?" asked the wasi.

Strong suspected he already knew the truth, and replied, "Do I sit in your tent?"

After gulping down gallons of water and eating some bread, Strong and Haraami rejoined Mack, Belsky, and Hardin at the security tent. None of the men mentioned what happened in the tomb to anybody. It would be too painful to mention. Besides, no one would believe them. With a new injury to complain about, Mack was in good spirits. When Strong walked in the tent door, Mack reached out and hugged him around the neck.

"My friend," he said, closing his eyes.

After hearing about (some) of the events from the burial chamber, he agreed with Strong. That night, they demolished the hidden staircase entrance to the Ten Guardians' tomb.

Later, Strong wrote to the families of Joel Killroy and Marcus Martell, mentioning their exemplary service and steadfast friendship. He attempted to contact the family of Stella von Strauss, but could not find any on record.

After weighing the risks of tomb raiding, Strong and his men decided it was time for a vacation. Belsky returned home to Austria to see his family and Greg Hardin went west to search for Nefertiti's golden tits.

"I want to see grass and trees again," Strong told Mack, the night after Belsky and Hardin departed.

They flipped a coin: heads for America, tails for England. The next day, they boarded a ship to New York City, where they would begin their week-long pub crawl.

Two weeks later, Carter and Lord Carnarvon broke the seal on Tut's tomb. Inside, they found the world's most well-preserved mummy and enough artifacts to keep egyptologists busy for the next century. Among the artifacts they found was a blunt dagger. Origin? Cosmic.

THE END

THE MYSTERY OF THE VOYNICH MANUSCRIPT

New York City, 1930

"**Y**ou big bastards," said Harvey Strong, staring up at a diorama of two Asian elephants.

The mated pair of elephants were a snapshot in time. They didn't move, but the way their legs and trunks were positioned, it seemed like they might come alive at any moment. Strong's gaze turned to the elephant closest to him and his eyes followed the large silhouette of the body up to the head. The beast's eyes stared blankly ahead into the darkness of the surrounding exhibits. The eyes were calm, almost as if the creature had accepted his fate long before being skinned, stuffed, and glued back together. He knew the eyes were glass, but he found comfort in them. Even in death, in seemed, there was some peace. Strong wondered if the beast had seen the shot coming or had been killed while eating, playing, or mating.

As Strong wondered about the land where the elephant had once inhabited, his mind wandered back to Egypt. Even eight years later, he could recall the feeling of sand in every pore of his body, the intense, baking sun at his back, and the consistent mumblings in Arabic. He decided he didn't miss it. Suddenly, his mind shifted to the vision of a woman clothed in white satin robes with long wavy blonde hair. He stifled the thoughts and continued his walk down the South Asiatic Hall, the newest exhibit and the first major hall of mammal habitat dioramas.

The American Museum of Natural History contained an immense amount of sewn carcasses, bottled specimens, and sand-free artifacts from around the globe. Its long halls, separated by geographical area, reminded Strong of the passageways of an Egyptian tomb. At night—as he had not seen them in the daylight—the darkness seemed to guard the creatures housed here. Strong would round a corner and catch a glimmer from a pair of cold, glassy eyes. He wasn't afraid of these eyes, but they made him uneasy. It seemed as if, at any moment, those eyes might blink or follow him down the hallway.

As nighttime security for the museum, Strong would canvas the entire museum, sit and sip on cold coffee for five minutes, and then do it all over again until day broke and he left to go home and sleep. He had already been six months on the job and was already bored out of his mind. As he walked the corridors, he would shine his flashlight in the directions of creaks and moans from dark corners of the hallways and exhibits, expecting to see someone jump out and attack him. They never did. The light would reveal a mouse, or a stray piece of paper, or nothing at all. Sometimes, he hoped for an armed intruder. That, thought Strong, would make for an interesting time, at least.

As he passed the silent Siberian tiger diorama and rounded the corner into the Books and Letters Exhibit, Strong saw something he had never seen in the museum before. Ahead of him, at the end of the hall, a light was shining out of one of the exhibit rooms to the right. He could tell it was the light of a flashlight much like his own, as the light beam danced on the hallway wall outside the room. Strong grabbed for something at his hip—a gun, a knife, or something—but there was nothing there.

"Security men," Albert Shue, his boss, had told him on the day he was hired, "don't carry weapons or engage in fights."

Strong was sitting across the desk in a chair, staring at Mr. Shue. He had inquired about carrying a pistol on the job. Hell, a knife would have been fine with Strong. No matter, he decided, Strong didn't expect anyone to try to steal from a museum. It was like stealing from a dead man: there's nothing of value left to take.

Mr. Shue squirmed in his seat, and said, "Out there—in the streets—people don't care what you do. Rob them blind, kick their children, or simply spit your gum on their shoe. They could care less, as long as they have what they want. In here, Mr. Strong, I don't care what you want. If you see something, do as I've told you: alert the police."

Strong agreed, if only to shut up Mr. Shue. Later that night, he wore the assigned uniform: khaki pants, a white shirt, and well-polished dress shoes. On his chest was pinned a brass badge, inscribed with the words: "Museum Security." In his hands was a metal flashlight with a dim bulb. He hoped, at least, that the light would last the night.

As Strong walked closer to the lit room at the end of the Books and Letters Exhibit, he thought about running back to the office, picking up the phone, and calling the police. It's what Mr. Shue would have wanted. It's what the police would have wanted. Yet, Strong decided, it wasn't what he wanted. If they would make him traipse around these light-forsaken halls with nothing but a brass button and a dim flashlight, he was going to make the most of the first—and probably only—chance he got to have some fun. He suspected it was some kid looking for pirate's gold or something to pawn off.

Strong snuck up to the door, shuffling his feet as quietly as possible, but the polished shoes he wore made one hell of a noise on the tile floors. Strong wondered if Mr. Shue did this to track Strong's whereabouts inside the museum. It didn't matter, Mr. Shue was sound asleep in his comfy bed in his Manhattan apartment by now. Strong clicked off his flashlight as his shoulder brushed against the door frame. He didn't want the intruder catching sight of his light and making a run for it. Strong counted, "One… two… three," and burst through the doorway.

As he ran, Strong made out the silhouette of a body and threw his weight against it. Whoever it was fell hard to the tile floor and his flashlight rolled across the room. It pointed on the wall and illuminated the silhouettes of the two people—Strong and the intruder—struggling for advantage on the floor. Strong was easily able to push down the intruder and used his weight to crush the person below.

"Stop! No, please! Oh God, help me!" Shouted the intruder.

Immediately, Strong assessed that it was a male and was from somewhere near Russia, by the accent placed on each syllable. Strong put his fingers around the Russian's throat. With the intruder secure, he reached over and picked up the flashlight. The light began to dim, so Strong shook it, and the beam came back to life. He pointed it in the face of his intruder.

He was an old man with a grey beard that came to a point a few inches below his chin, and a patch of gray hair on each side of his head. Strong guessed that he was fifty or sixty, at least. He looked skinny, obviously not the type that had spent his working years lifting boulders and shoveling dirt or sand. He looked like a professor or magistrate.

"What are you doing in here?" Strong asked, shoving his arm down into his neck and making the man cough.

"I—I—I am looking for something," replied the man, grabbing onto Strong's forearm with both hands to try and release the pressure from his neck.

Strong realized the man was no threat. If anything, he was a thief, but not one that would put up a fight. The old man knew he was defeated and Strong let go of his neck.

"Thank—thank you," said the old man, in his Russian accent.

Strong jumped to his feet and made sure the flashlight was still on his captive. He had seen men of seventy take off in a split second. They didn't last long, but, for old men, they had a few good bursts of speed left in them. The captive slowly lifted himself to a sitting position, groaning with each movement. Feeling a little remorse for his tackle, Strong offered his arm and helped the man to his feet. The old man bent over and picked up a set of glasses from the floor and put them on his face. Strong noticed he had cracked both lenses. He felt worse.

"What's your name?" Strong inquired, looking around to see what the man had been after.

"Wilfrid Voynich, but my friends call me Willy," he said, sniffling his nose and stretching out one of his legs.

"Voynich, huh? You Russian?" Asked Strong, moving the flashlight up the man's body to check for weapons and to make an assessment about him. He noticed Willy was wearing a gray wool suit, much like a professor would wear.

"My family is Polish, but we are—were—a part of the Russian Empire, unfortunately," he said, spitting onto the floor.

"Okay—well, what the hell are you doing in here? I could have called the police or even killed you."

Willy turned and Strong quickly grabbed his arm to prevent his escape. Voynich stopped and said, "Let me show you."

Strong released Willy's arm and the old man shuffled to a glass case against the wall. Willy stopped when he got to the case and tried to look into it. The darkness hid it, so he motioned for Strong to point his flashlight. The light illuminated a cache of parchments, books, and letters inside the case.

"Books. Are you trying to steal one in particular or the whole bunch?" Asked Strong, pointing the flashlight into Willy's face. The light refracted off his glasses.

"I would never steal from a museum, sir," said Willy, puffing out his chest, "But I couldn't wait until the museum opened on Monday to see the page."

Strong knew that if he asked "why" then he was moving further and further away from the new life he had taken on. Mr. Shue would already have this man in cuffs and hauled away to jail. The police would question him tomorrow, long after whatever thing that made this man in such a hurry had occurred.

Just in case, Strong asked, "Why?"

Willy looked at Strong in the face. "They will be here soon."

"Who?"

At that moment, the sharp sound of glass breaking entered the room. From inside, Strong couldn't deduce where the sound had come from, but he knew it wasn't good. Before he could ask Willy again, the old man raised his arm and smashed his elbow down through the glass. He reached in, carefully, and pulled out leather-bound book. Strong was amazed.

"Shine that torch over here," commanded Willy.

Strong found himself following the command.

The light revealed the book's title, "Secretum Secretorum," written in a large, gilded font. Below, the author: Doctor Mirabilis. Willy smiled and opened the book. He thumbed through the large, ancient parchment pages. Some illustrations and drawings adorned the text-filled pages. Willy stopped on a page that looked to contain some sort of cipher wheel. He carefully ran his fingers across the page, caressing the edge of the page ever so slightly, and then ripped it out.

"Hey! What are you doing?" Strong said, grabbing the old man by the shoulder again.

"No time to be careful, Mister…"

"Strong."

"Mr. Strong. I can't explain at the moment, but we really must get out of here. You are unarmed and, I'm afraid, I can't say the same about the others."

Strong wasn't going to waste time asking more questions. If he had learned anything during his time in the army and on adventures across the world, it was to shoot-first and ask questions later. With a brass badge and flashlight, he decided neither of those options were appropriate at the moment. He grabbed Willy's arm and pulled him out into the hall. Willy shoved the torn page into his coat pocket.

Strong looked down each hallway, but didn't hear movement. Yet, as he peered down the hallway from where he had just recently walked, he saw the faint beams of light dancing off the wall. From the look of the dancing lights, it seemed there might be five or six people running down the hallway toward them. Strong's eyes widened and he grabbed Willy's arm again.

"We gotta go," he tugged the old man town the opposite hallway from the lights.

The two men ran as fast as they could down the Books and Letters Exhibit, passed into the Ocean Life Exhibit, and came to the rotunda in the Grand Gallery.

"My bike is parked outside," said Strong, pointing to the doorway that opened into West 77th Street. The headlights of cars could be seen through the windows.

Just as they stepped forward, the doors burst open and three men walked through. The first was tall and wearing a black suit. His beard was pointed at his chin, like Willy's, but was still black with youth. He wore a black hat on his head and Strong could tell that a pistol was tucked into his pants at his right hip from the bulge that pressed against his jacket. The other two men wore plain trousers and shirts. Yet, in their hands were "Chicago Typewriters," the Thompson submachine gun, a favorite of mobsters and bootleggers. They pointed them at Strong and Willy.

The man in the black suit spoke up in Russian, "*Dayte mne, chto eto moye, i vy mozhete poyti.*"

Before Strong could reply, Willy made a mad dash down the hallway. The man in the black suit looked surprised, as did his enforcers. Strong looked back at the enforcers and the man in the black suit, then back in Willy's direction. For a moment, he contemplated giving himself up, but assumed that he didn't have what they wanted—whatever it was. Figuring he was dead anyway, he scampered after Willy. Immediately, his shadow was riddled with bullet holes as Strong disappeared down the hallway. The man in the black suit ordered his men to give chase.

Strong ran down the New York State Environment Hall, passing beavers, deer and otters as he tried to catch up to Willy. After a moment, he realized that he didn't even hear Willy's footsteps ahead of him, so he stopped running. He turned around and looked for the old man, and saw Willy motioning to him from a dark corner.

"Mr. Strong—over here. We must use the darkness to our advantage," Willy slid over to make room for Strong, who was double his size.

They pushed their bodies together and completely disappeared into the darkness of the corner. A moment later, two enforcers carrying Thompsons passed them without notice. Willy motioned for Strong to move out into the hallway and then Willy ran back toward the way they had come.

"Wait—what about the others that were chasing us, back in the Books and Letters Exhibit?" Strong asked.

Willy shouted as he ran, "Your bike…it's our only chance!"

Strong followed and the two ran back toward the door. The man in the black suit wasn't there, but a group of men carrying flashlights were running down the hall in their direction. The darkness hid them from view, but when the lights hit their bodies, someone called out something in Russian. Immediately, guns fired and bullets whizzed around Strong's head. He ducked and swerved, but kept running, following Willy's lead. With each step, it seemed like the men with guns would reach them before they reached the door. Yet, right in the knick of time, Willy sharply turned and they busted out of the front doors and into the street.

Cars blew past them and Strong motioned for Willy to follow him around the side of the front steps. Willy followed behind and they soon arrived at Strong's bike—a 1931 Harley-Davidson 730cc, Model D. Strong mounted the bike and tried to kick it to life. Willy jumped onto the back of the bike and sat on the back fender. After a third kick, the engine of the motorcycle roared to life. Strong switched on the headlight and pulled back the throttle just as a group of enforcers busted through the front door of the museum. They looked around to try to find their prey, but didn't see them in the darkness. Strong and Willy plunged forward into the street. The sound of the engine got the attention of the enforcers, who attempted to shoot the men from the bike. A spray of bullets whizzed past Strong and Willy. The men narrowly escaped death, a bullet nicking Strong's handlebars. The bike sped forward and, before long, they were out of sight and bullet range. They turned down a side street, hardly slowing to make the turn.

Willy shouted in Strong's ear, "Where are we going?"

Strong turned his head and hollered back, "To see an old friend of mine."
"Who?"
"Mack Thatcher."

"I can't believe you, Harvey! I really can't. You get shot at, multiple times, and decide to bring your trail of lead to my doorstep! What in God's name were you thinking? Did it not occur to you that maybe—just maybe—that I'm done with that life. We made a deal that…"

Mack wasn't happy seeing Strong. Sure, they met nightly at *Ricardo's*, a local hole-in-the-wall that had enough balls to serve dark liquor. Yet, it had been a while—years even—since Strong had brought danger to Mack's doorstep. When they arrived in New York in '22, they made the town squeal for mercy with their binge drinking and partying. Hell, they even found their way into some trouble now and again. Mack would join in, as he always did, just as soon as he would quit his banter.

"Mack—Mack, please. Mack, I know—Look," was all Strong could get in edgewise.

Willy Voynich sat staring at his torn piece of parchment in the living room. Strong could tell he was having a hard time reading it with both of his glasses lens broken.

"I knew this would happen again soon. I told myself, 'Mack, you gotta tell Harvey to get back in the saddle and find himself another or he'll,'" murmured Mack, motioning as if he was talking to a mirror.

Harvey watched on in agony. He probably needed to hear it, but he didn't have time right now. The man in the black suit, and his enforcers with their Thompsons, would find them soon enough. While he had parked the bike a few blocks away from Mack's apartment, Strong didn't underestimate the power of evil men. Not anymore. He decided it was time to get a word in.

"Mack!" Strong shouted at the top of his lungs. Mack stopped talking and stared at Strong in astonishment. "Look…"

"And now you yell at me in my own home? What has gotten into you?" asked Mack, walking to the kitchen.

Strong followed him, watching him pull a dusty glass from the cupboard and filling it up with brandy. The liquid was the color of amber and Mack downed it without a wince.

"Mack, I'm sorry. I completely understand your frustration," Strong used his hands to convey his sincerity, "But, this is different. This mess fell into my lap. Now, if you just hear me out, I…"

"Who is he?" Asked Mack, pointing to Willy in the living room.

"Voyner—Voystig—Something Russian or Prussian, or something. I caught him trying to steal something from the museum and then guns started blazing around us. He's an old man so I saved his ass. I don't know…"

"I think I was the one doing the ass saving, as you put it," said Willy, who had crept up behind them.

Strong turned and stared at him. His suit was mangled by the gunfight and the bike ride, but he didn't look phased in the least.

Willy walked up to Mack and put out his hand, saying, "My name is Wilfrid Voy—nich," sounding out his last name to help the men pronounce it. "And, as Mr. Strong here almost had it, I am Polish. We must require your help."

Mack slowly shook the old man's hand. Then, he said, "I like you. You've got grit, I can tell. Name's Mack Thatcher. Proud Englishman and world traveler. I can hold my own, unlike my friend here."

Strong rolled his eyes. The three men got drinks and sat at the dining room table. Mack cleared the old plates of food and newspapers to find the wood beneath them. Willy removed his glasses and rubbed his eyes.

"I am a book seller, gentlemen," Willy related. "And I have been since I left Siberia. I arrived in London and began my business there in '98. Life for my wife, Ethel, and I was good for some years. In '05 or '06, a man approached me, asking about a mysterious book. As was my business, I agreed to search out this book for him. A few years later, I succeeded in doing so. In fact, as fate would have it, the book entered my shop and the seller wanted to sell it for a reasonable price. Unfortunately, this seller told me that a man was trying to kill him and take the book. The man he described was the same man that I was employed by. In fact, he is the same man that we saw tonight at the museum, Mr. Strong."

Mack and Strong were entranced by the tale. Strong spoke up, "Who is he? I heard him speak Russian."

"Yes, he is Russian," Willy concurred. "His name is Yuri Stronovich. If that is his true name, I don't know, but that's the one he gave to me upon our first meeting. Anyways, after hearing the seller's tale about Mr. Stronovich's attempt on his life, I was sure that this task I had undertaken wasn't the way of decency. I am a good man—of strong faith and values. I don't hurt, nor do I kill. If I serve evil, it is only because I didn't know evil when it shook my hand. So, I did the only thing I could do."

"What?" asked Mack.

"I bought the book and have been running from Stronovich ever since. It has been nearly fifteen years since I last saw him, but I knew he would find me, eventually. Even in America, you cannot hide forever." Willy adjusted his glasses. He pulled off his tie and unbuttoned his top shirt button.

"This book—what is it?" asked Strong.

"Yeah—does it have value?" inquired Mack.

"No—none, whatsoever," Willy replied. Mack looked disappointed. "Yet, it may hold secrets just yet."

"Secrets," repeated Strong, "what do you mean?"

"Well, for the longest time I didn't even open the book. I feared that what it contained might be the work of evil. However, it is not. Inside are drawings—fantastical and curious—and the text, well, the text is unreadable. It is in a language that does not exist."

"Then, what the hell good is it to us?" queried Mack.

"None," said Willy, "without this." He pulled the torn piece of paper from his coat pocket and laid it on the table. "In my research, I have come to conclude that this manuscript, that Stronovich wants for his own, is the work of Doctor Mirabilis."

"Doctor Mirabilis? That's what was on the book you tore that page from," Strong remembered from back in the museum. He wondered what Mr. Shue would think of the bullet-riddled museum when he arrived in the morning. It didn't matter now.

Willy explained: "Yes, Doctor Mirabilis—meaning "wondrous doctor"—is the scholastic name of Roger Bacon, the 13th century English philosopher and friar. Anyways, among the usual sciences and philosophies, Bacon was also an alchemist and was often associated with the supernatural and magical arts. Obvious falsehoods, but this manuscript is interesting, to say the least. The text is jumbled in an unknown order and the drawings and sketches seem to be of a place that does not exist. At first, I assumed it to be a fake, or maybe a joke by the wondrous doctor. However, after seeing this page in Bacon's other book, *Secretum Secretorum*, and that the language matched the language in the manuscript, I knew it must be a cipher to decode the manuscript's language."

"Well—what are we waiting for? Let's get the manuscript and see what that thing says!" Mack shouted, slamming down his empty glass.

"Wait, wait, wait. Hold on a minute," said Strong. "What makes you think this manuscript is worth your life?"

"I don't know, for sure, Mr. Strong. Yet, the philologist I have been working with for some time on this manuscript assures me that Bacon didn't write tricks or riddles. His works were purely scientific and always accurate. The subject of his manuscript must be very secretive, for some reason, because he had to use a ciphered language," said Willy. "And, Mr. Thatcher, I agree with you completely. I say we run over Ms. Newsome's office and use this cipher immediately!"

"I knew it must be a cipher..."

Strong's eyes widened and he stared up at the wall. If ever there was a name is wished not to here at this moment, it was Ms. Newsome.

"Newsome," Strong cleared his throat. "As in Cate Newsome, the philologist?"

The moment Willy shook his head in approval, Strong leaned back and let out a groan. Mack smiled and began laughing.

"What's the joke? Is Ms. Newsome not respected in your circle of friends?" asked Willy, not comprehending the joke.

"No, my friend," said Mack, "Ms. Newsome is Mr. Strong's former ladylove."

It was true. In '28, Mack had met Cate at the museum. At that time, he didn't work there, but was interested in the exhibit on Egyptian hieroglyphics, having seen them up close and personal on more than one occasion. Cate was a philologist, expert in ancient languages, and was giving a talk on the exhibit's artifacts. When he saw her, she impressed him with her intelligence and poise. She knew something about everything. That night, they spent hours talking at a local restaurant and—months later—shared an apartment together. Mack told him that she was his match: beautiful, intelligent, and willing to put up with his adventurous nature. Unfortunately, after he came home one night drunk and covered in blood, Cate decided she had enough of Harvey Strong. She left him the next day and they hadn't spoken since. That was all nearly a year ago.

"Well, Ms. Newsome has the manuscript at her office, so we don't have a choice. In fact, seeing as they found me at the museum, I fear that she might be in danger. After all, Stronovich is a resourceful man. If he found me, as careful as I am, a renowned philologist won't be hard to locate," Willy reasoned.

With Cate's safety in mind, the three men loaded into Mack's car to drive to her office across town. In the least, they would get the manuscript. Mack's car, a Buick Series 40 of unknown year, cranked along down the freeway towards Cate's office. In the back seat, Willy was still examining the torn page from *Secretem Secretorum*. The drive from Manhattan to Queens was quick, and they arrived at Cate's second-story office space within twenty minutes. Her building was made of brick and looked as if it had been around since the gangs of New York ran the place. Strong remembered Cate's father was in real estate. They exited the car and rang the buzzer for the office. After a few tries, and no answer, Mack picked the lock and they were inside.

Mack turned to Willy and said, "I bet your books don't teach you that."

Willy began a response, but Strong and Mack were already halfway up the stairs. Quickly, he scurried after them.

Cate had rented the office space while she was living with Strong. Up until then, she did her research in the house, but found she could focus better at a separate office. The three men walked through the dark office spaces until they found one labeled: "Catherine Newsome, Philology." To their dismay, the glass was broken and the door was left unlocked and swinging open. Strong pushed ahead of Mack and burst into the room. Inside, the office was empty. Her desk had been rummaged through and papers strewn everywhere. The window was open and wind from the street outside was blowing the papers around the room. Strong lifted an overturned lamp and set it on its base.

"She's gone," Strong sat on her desk. He put his head down, wishing he had been here earlier. He wished he had done a lot of things differently.

Mack put his arm on Strong's shoulder. "We'll find her, buddy. She's a smart girl."

Willy began looking through Cate's things, as if he knew what he was looking for. Strong and Mack watched him dig through file after file. With no luck, he began on her filing cabinet. Nothing. Frustrated, he stopped and stared out the window into the night.

Mack looked up and noticed a broken ceiling panel. "Hell, they even busted the ceiling."

Immediately, Willy looked up and smiled, as if he experienced an epiphany. He grabbed Cate's desk chair and pulled it to the center of the room. He counted three tiles to the left and four tiles down with his finger, then pushed the tile up and let it fall to the ground. He reached his hand in and pulled out a large book with a very faded cover. It was the manuscript.

"How did you..?" began Strong, but Willy cut him off.

"Cate and I planned for an event like this. She knew all about Stronovich and the mystery of the manuscript. She was smart, but not smart enough to stay away from me," Willy explained.

Strong shook his head, thinking the same about himself.

"We were always interested in page 34 because of an illustration it has on it of a volcano. We decided to hide it in the ceiling if anything happened and use 3-4 as a cipher to find it quickly." Willy wiped dust off the manuscript and tucked it under his arm.

Strong and Mack agreed that they would go to Strong's apartment in Manhattan to retrieve "necessaries." As they drove back down the freeway, a book-heavier than before, Strong stared at the blacktop ahead. He wondered if Cate was all right and what she looked like now. He looked in the side mirror and saw headlights behind them.

"Ya know, I haven't seen Cate in probably eight months," said Mack, breaking the silence.

"Eight months, huh," repeated Strong. "I haven't seen her in over a year now. Where'd you see her?"

"As a matter of fact, it was at *Ricardo's*. She came in looking for you. She told me not to tell you she did. I figure now, with her life at stake, I could break that promise." Mack kept his eyes on the road as he spoke.

Strong turned his eyes from the headlights in the side mirror to the road ahead. The black asphalt freeway was full of holes and loose gravel. He was glad Mack wasn't speeding. These cars had no give and men were often crushed in accidents. He didn't ride in cars much, preferring the open-air luxury of his motorcycle. He thought about Cate; about their last argument. She wanted him to take a steady job and be home more often. He agreed, but found it hard to be cooped up anywhere for too long. He often blamed the war. He had been a POW after being injured at the Siege of Antwerp. Cate didn't buy his excuse. She loved him—and he loved her—but their lives, it seemed, were on different paths. The distance between their paths grew thin during the good years, but the distance became too great for them to hold on to each other.

Mack took the exit off the freeway and turned toward Strong's apartment. From Cate's office in Queens, Manhattan seemed like hundreds of miles away. Darkness has that effect, Strong thought. It reminded him of the hours he spent walking the dark halls of the museum. Those hours seemed like days, most of the time. He looked in the rearview, noticing the same headlights behind them. Immediately, he perked up and looked behind him.

"We've got a tail," he said, matter-of-factly.

Both Mack and Willy looked behind them. After taking an unnecessary turn, the car behind them followed and they agreed they had a tail. Mack slammed his foot on the gas pedal and the Buick roared to life. He swerved left around the median and began driving on the wrong side of the road.

"What are you doing?" shouted Strong, holding on to the dashboard with both hands.

"We'll see what Stronovich's men are made of." Mack swerved back around the median. The car behind them was trying to keep up, but Mack's errant driving made it difficult.

Immediately, another car appeared out of a side street and slammed into the side of Mack's Buick. The car took the brunt of the hit and was sent skidding sideways until it hit an oak tree in the median and came to stop. All three men had been jostled during the crash, with Strong and Mack pushed against the driver-side door and Willy upside down in the floorboard. As he came to, Strong wished there was sort of rope or belt to keep people in place while driving. He felt blood gushing out of the side of his right arm and looked down to see a gash near his elbow. The passenger door was caved in. Willy was scrambling out of the open window and Strong motioned to Mack to do the same.

All three men made it out just in time to hear the retraction of machine gun bolts. They looked up and saw a group of six men exiting their vehicles, Thompsons pointed at them. Strong then heard the click of two pistols beside him. Mack pulled his guns from the shoulder holsters. When Strong turned and saw the pistols, Mack smiled.

Out of the car stepped the man in the black suit, Yuri Stronovich. Strong recognized his black, pointed beard and the bulge of a pistol at his hip. Behind Stronovich was a much smaller, more beautiful figure. It was Cate. An enforcer of Stronovich pushed her out of the car and pointed his pistol at her stomach. Strong started to run toward her, but the Thompsons in his face kept him from doing it. Stronovich walked the middle ground between the enforcers and Strong's crew.

"Well, well, well. What do we have here?" Stonovich spoke in English with a heavy Russian accent, "Wilfrid Voynich, my old friend. And—what's this—I see you have finally found my book!"

Voynich quickly retorted, "This will never be your book, Stronovich. You have no honor and are a ruthless killer!"

"Maybe you're right, Mr. Voynich, but I paid you to do a job and you have done it. Now, hand it over."

Willy reached in his coat, slightly scaring the armed men standing across from them. He pulled out his wallet and threw it at Stronovich.

"There, you blood-sucker! Have all you want," said Willy.

Strong was impressed by the old man's tenacity.

"I don't need money, Mr. Voynich, I never have. I have the map and now I have the book that contains the latitudinal and longitudinal directions. I don't even need a translator, now," said Stronovich, pulling his pistol, a brand new Tokarev, and pointing it at Cate.

"No! Wait!" Strong stepped forward. "Take me, Stronovich. Leave her be."

Stronovich smirked, then hollered out, "Then give me the book!"

Strong walked over to Willy and pried the book from his unwilling hands. Willy lowered his head, defeated. Strong walked up to Stronovich and handed the book to him. Strong had underestimated Stronovich's figure, as he must have stood at least six-foot, four-inches and weighed over two hundred pounds. Strong stepped back, never taking his eyes off Cate. A hammer cocked behind Strong. He turned and saw an enforcer holding a pistol to Mack's head. Mack lowered his pistols and dropped them on the ground.

"Now," said Stronovich, "I could just kill you and be done with it. But, I have my book, and, for that, I will spare your lives. Follow me and you will die."

The enforcers lowered their guns and walked back to the cars. They left the crashed vehicle blocking Mack's Buick. Before getting into the car, Stronovich turned and walked back to the three men like he had forgotten something.

"This is for making me wait," Stronovich said grimly, raising his pistol and firing a shot directly at Willy. The shot hit the old man right in the center of his chest and he fell backward onto the ground. Cate pulled free from her captor and ran to him, shouting his name. Strong cursed at Stronovich.

Stronovich re-holstered his pistol and stepped into the car. The cars squealed out and disappeared into the night. Mack picked up his pistols. Cate was on her knees, holding Willy's head off the ground. Blood covered the front of his suit and was leaking onto the sidewalk. Cate began sobbing.

"Cate—please, don't cry for me," said Willy, in a voice that suddenly revealed his years and mileage. "You must go on…"

Willy pulled the torn piece of paper from his coat pocket and handed it to Cate. As she took it, he grabbed her hand and squeezed it tightly.

"You can do this, Cate, I know you can," Willy uttered with his final words, and in a moment, he was gone.

Cate slowly placed his head on the sidewalk, lowered her head and cried. Strong made a motion toward her, but Mack stepped in his way.

"Not right now, my friend," Mack whispered. "She needs time before she sees another pain."

Mack grabbed Cate around the shoulder and led her away from the accident. Police sirens slowly approached toward them, so they snuck down a back alley and boarded the subway. On the train, Cate sat silent, clutching the paper Willy had given to her.

"Lincoln Road, to Manhattan," said Strong, "Are we getting off?"

"No," replied Cate, looking up at him for the first time. He looked into her green eyes, the same shade as his own. Her mascara was running down her cheeks and the whites of her eyes were red.

"Why? Where should we go? The police?" asked Mack.

"No," Cate said again. "We need to go to Ecuador."

"Ecuador?" Mack shifted his body toward her.

"I heard Stronovich's men talking in the car. They were discussing tickets they had bought from Newark Liberty Airport to Ecuador. They have some map that me and Willy didn't know about. It must lead to Ecuador," Cate sighed. The sound of Willy's name visibly haunted her.

"Cate—We don't know if that's where they're going for sure, we don't have plane tickets, or money to get any, and, besides, Willy's gone, Cate," Strong said.

She looked at him in the eyes. "That's exactly why we need to go. Willy and I have researched that manuscript for damn near a year now and I won't stop because Stronovich decided Willy's life wasn't worth a damn book!"

"It was, Cate," said Strong. Cate and Mack looked up at him. "Willy was one of the most wily and courageous old men I've ever met. The way he cared for you—I know that feeling. Let's do this, for him."

Mack shook his head, "What have I gotten myself into?"

Cate stared at Strong, but didn't smile. Strong sensed that she wanted to hug him. He wanted the same, but they didn't.

"Let's get our gear rounded up and meet at Newark Liberty in two hours," suggested Strong.

They all agreed. Mack protested when Cate left on her own, but Strong assured him she was tough enough to handle herself.

Some time later, the subway screeched to a halt and they exited at Newark Libery Airport. Strong was carrying a canvas duffle bag and a suitcase, Mack carried a simple leather overnight bag, and Cate had a suitcase and a document folder. They pooled together their money—Cate had the most—and bought three tickets to Quito, Ecuador.

A day later, the three stepped off the plane into the capital city of Quito. Strong and Mack had talked most of the way to Quito, between drinks. Cate sat silent in her window seat, staring out over the massive expanse of water and land that their plane passed over. Strong could tell she was coming to terms with Willy's death and was better left alone.

When they arrived in Quito, Mack secured their accommodations at a local hotel. It wasn't a five-star joint, but it had beds with clean linens and an all night bar. Cate said goodnight and left for her room upstairs, leaving Mack and Strong in the bar for some rest.

"Ya know, bud, this is the first time we've been out of your country in damn near two years!" Mack threw back a shot of tequila. He coughed once and returned to his cigarette.

"Yeah—what was it? Antilla?" Strong raised his glass of whisky and took a sip.

"Antilla? No—that was in '25 or '26. I'm talking about '27, the year the Yankees swept the Pirates," Mack corrected.

"Oh, I remember that year. The year of Lindbergh," Strong added. "I think we were in Greece."

Mack agreed and the two shared a few tales remembering their old adventures. Strong recalled a few silver coins he still had in his apartment, which made Mack jealous. After a final round, Strong decided it was time for some shut eye. If they were going after Stronovich in the morning, they needed all the help they could get. He caressed the knife on his hip and said good night to Mack, who ordered his "final" drink.

Strong walked up the stairs slowly, taking in the warm air of Quito as he did. He felt like his blood was warm again, chasing something down and risking it all. He remembered Cate telling him—a year ago now—that his adventures would cost him his life. He told her that he had lost things worth more than his life already, so what did he have to fear?

As Strong rounded the corner to his hall, Cate bumped right into him. She was carrying a bucket full of ice and was covered in a white robe. Her hair—burgundy and straight—was shoulder length and curled a little at the ends. He hadn't seen her hair like that in years.

"Harvey—I..." she began, but stopped herself. She pushed past him and continued walking in the direction of her room.

"Cate—wait, please."

Cate stopped and turned around slowly. She hesitated for a moment, but then dropped her eyes slowly and tears fell from them. Harvey moved in closer to her, but paused before embracing her. She slowly moved toward him and he grabbed her, wrapping his arms around her body and squeezing her tight. He felt the warmth between them. She dropped the bucket of ice and wrapped her arms around him.

"Cate, I'm so sorry about what happened to Willy. He was a good..." said Harvey, but Cate cut him off.

"No, Harvey, I'm sorry about what happened to *us*," said Cate, looking up at him.

Strong didn't know how to respond. He had not expected her to even be thinking about him, let alone their relationship.

"It's been the worst year of my life. Had it not been for Willy and his manuscript, I would have gone crazy," she confessed.

"I've missed you," Strong admitted.

"I've missed you, too," Cate echoed.

The pair slowly met at the lips and didn't stop until another couple walked by them. They separated and allowed the couple to pass them by. Cate grabbed Strong by the hand and led him to her room. There he stayed until the sunlight peeked over the horizon and found its way through the opening between the curtains.

They met Mack downstairs for breakfast.

"People all morning been trying to sell me watches, newspapers, and old news," said Mack, sipping from his steaming coffee cup. He had a plate of eggs in front of him.

"I wish we had some news about Stronovich. You said you had a boy on that?" Strong sipped from a cup of coffee, as well.

"Yeah—Darwin, he calls himself. I told him to look for a large white man in a black suit being accompanied by some bad looking men."

"Well, I hope that works. Without the manuscript, this cipher page is worthless," said Cate, taking a bite of toast.

For a moment, they all ate in silence. They stared out of the balcony into the jungle, where mountains rose from the treetops in the distance.

Mack swallowed and coffee and spoke up, "Oh—yeah, I forgot to tell you. Darwin—the boy I have looking for Stronovich—was telling me about a volcano nearby."

Strong nodded. "I remember Willy saying something about that." He turned to Cate.

"Volcano—yes," she said, "There is a page in the manuscript—page 34—that has what looks to be a volcano. We always found that page interesting because it seemed to be part of an incomplete map."

"Didn't Stronovich say he had a map, and all he needed was the manuscript to find the location?" asked Strong.

"If he has a complete map, part of which contains the figure of a volcano, and it leads him here to Ecuador, then…" Cate stopped.

"Then it must be the volcano here," Strong completed her thought.

Mack looked at Strong and Cate in awe at their newfound camaraderie. He suspected "foul play."

"Mack," Cate queried, "Where is that volcano?"

Mack stood up. "About a day's ride south."

"Wait," said Cate, "We can't go there without knowing a bit of what we're getting into."

"What do you mean?" Strong asked.

"I'm going to the library to dig up some information on that volcano and his history. It's intertwined with the manuscript in some way. You two need to get our guide and gear ready. Can you do that?" Cate had a fire in her eyes. Strong recognized it as the look she got when she was curious.

"Two hours?" Asked Mack.

They all agreed on the time and departed the cafe. Mack and Strong went to town, where they secured a guide and horses for the journey. Mack suspected that Stronovich had the resources to get to the volcano by jeep. It didn't matter. They didn't have the funds and would have to make do with the horses. They rounded up their gear and managed to find a mercantile with the

"We can't go there without knowing..."

right ammunition for their weapons. Strong had his trusty Henry Repeater and Mack was carrying his pistols. When they finished the preparations, they sat in the hotel bar and drank waters. Earlier, they found it too hot in Quito to drink all day without dying of dehydration. A half hour later, Cate arrived with a large book under her arm.

"I managed to convince the librarian that an American philologist who has received numerous distinguished awards wouldn't leave the city with one of her books," said Cate, throwing the tome down on the bar top. "I felt so bad lying to her."

"Either way—what did you find out? What is this book?" Strong slid the book his way to get a better look at the title.

Cate pulled the book back her way, "It's very old, so be careful with it. It's called *Natural y astrológico Historia del Ecuador*—which translates to 'Natural and Astrological History of Ecuador.' It was published in the early part of the 1600s, when Ecuador was under Spanish rule. This book recorded the local history of natural and astrological events: great floods, earthquakes, and volcanoes."

"Does it have our volcano?" Asked Mack.

"Well, there are quite a few volcanoes in this region, so it made it difficult to discern which was ours. Without modern maps or the use of common place names, I sifted through pages for hours," said Cate.

"So?" Strong was becoming impatient.

"So, I narrowed it down to three: Chakana, Cayambe, and Quilotoa. The first two were uneventful and really had no extenuating circumstances. However, the third, Quilotoa, erupted in the mid-1200s. Quilotoa's eruption left a large crater lake just south of Quito. That could be it." She turned to the page that wrote about Quilotoa and pointed to it.

"Let's get our gear and head out, then," said Mack.

"Wait," Strong held up his hand. "I've got to know something. Let's say this Quilotoa is the volcano in the manuscript. What is Roger Bacon, a 12th century philosopher, doing writing about an Ecuadorian volcano?"

Cate paused for a moment, contemplating her next words. Then, she said, "Willy had a theory. There is a decade in Bacon's life—roughly 1250-1260—where no one knew where he was or what he was doing. He theorized that Bacon somehow, for some reason, ended up at Quilotoa when, or right after, it erupted. During that time, the area was full of various native federations. It would have been highly dangerous and he might have been the first white man they had ever seen. Anyway, Willy's theory was that the manuscript was a record of what he had found at Quilotoa."

"Didn't Willy say the manuscript is full of jumbled writing and weird illustrations?" Reminded Mack.

"Yes," Cate replied, "It is. The writing is either ciphered, like we believe, or purely a hoax to keep people off the trail. The illustrations are odd; however, as they seem to show people, places, plants, and animals that would be new to the world as we know it. The plants and animals might have all gone extinct by now, and the people may have died of disease during the Spanish invasion, but Willy thought the manuscript was a record of a lost, mythical city."

"Wow," said Strong, "So Stronovich knows this?"

"I'm afraid he's the one who knew it first. Apparently, this is his life's mission. Willy and I only knew as much as we could gather from the manuscript."

"So we're heading to the last known location of a mythical city full of unknown people and animals—great," Strong said sarcastically.

"And Stronovich might have prepared better for this as he knows that we are getting into," Mack rationalized.

"Either way, we know our location and Stronovich might already be there. We need to get moving," Cate urged.

Strong and Mack agreed. After they grabbed their gear, they met Jose, their guide, and the horses that would carry them Quilotoa. Strong told Jose where they were going and the man shrugged, saying that there wasn't anything there worth seeing. They loaded on their horses and headed south down the main trail. Jeep tracks had dug two deep trenches in the mud trail and the horses were forced to walk on either side.

"*Pendejos. Estos turistas desgarran nuestros senderos,*" mumbled Jose under his breath.

Three hours later, Jose led the three travelers to a small river on the side of the trail. They dismounted and let the horses drink for a while and rest up. As Mack and Jose "spoke"—which was Mack talking in English and Jose acting like he was listening—Cate walked up to Strong, who was stroking his horse's mane.

"You two make a good couple," Cate smiled.

Strong always loved her smile, especially when she was neck deep in some ancient book and had found what she was looking for.

"Yeah, well, she doesn't argue as much as you did," Strong tried to make it obvious he was joking.

Cate was silent for a few moments. She stood on the other side of Strong's horse as it drank. It was a brown mare with a dark brown mane and tail. Cate patted the horse on the neck and it lifted its head from the water to check out Cate. Satisfied that Cate was no threat, the horse returned its mouth the water.

"Last night, I—we," said Strong.

"It wasn't anything, Harvey," said Cate. Strong looked at her quickly. He wondered why she had said that.

"So you and Willy had been working together since we split?" Asked Strong.

"Don't worry, he was more like a father."

"That's not what I meant."

"I know, I was joking. But, yes, we had been working for some time on the manuscript. I think he sensed his days were numbered. He wanted me to carry on the legacy.".

"Like the father you never had?"

"In a way, yes," Cate nodded. "He was a good man. His poor wife was always alone, but she understood who he was."

"That's a rare trait in a woman."

"Harvey..." Cate started but cut herself off. Changing the subject, she said, "What have you been doing this past year? Dubai? Greece, again? Egypt, perhaps?"

Strong smiled and laughed, "No. Egypt? Never again. Greece, maybe. But no, I have a job now."

"A job? Harvey Strong? Really?"

"Yes—I work for the museum."

"Which one? Not the American?" Cate asked, in disbelief.

"Yep. Nighttime security for the past six months."

"How is it?"

"Pure hell."

Jose called them back to begin again. Mack was already mounted on his black stallion and was ready to go. Mack helped Cate onto her horse and then mounted his own. He adjusted his Stetson and slightly kicked his mount. They took off down the trail south.

After hours of riding, they finally arrived near Quilotoa Crater Lake. A small scattering of buildings was in plain view across a small ridge and the edge of the crater could be seen just north. Jose turned his horse to look at the three travelers.

"*Aquí estamos,*" said Jose, "*Hay un pequeño hostal de enfrente. Sus compañeros ya han llegado.*"

Mack and Strong looked at each other. Neither of them knew Spanish, but Strong managed to catch the word "hostel" in there somewhere. Cate, a master of languages, understood Jose exactly. She turned to Mack and Strong.

"You can probably see the edges of the Quilotoa Crater ahead. He said there's a hostel up ahead."

"Great," Mack kicked his horse. "Let's go!"

Cate stopped him, saying, "He also said our 'companions' are already here."

"What does that mean?" Mack queried.

"Stronovich," Strong surmised.

"*¿Nuestros compañeros: cuántos han llegado?*" Cate asked of Jose.

Jose paused, counting, "*Cerca de una docena. Cuatro camiones llenos.*"

Cate translated. "He says there's about twelve of them. They took four jeeps to get here. They must have been the ones who tore up the road."

Strong spoke up, "Ask him about Stronovich."

Cate turned to Jose. "*¿Has visto nuestro amigo ruso? Él usaría ropa fina y dar órdenes.*"

"*¿Ruso?*" Jose began, "*Oh, sí, yo lo vi. hombre muy grande. Lleva un libro con él en todo momento.*"

"He says Stronovich is here, and he carries a larger book with him wherever he goes."

With all the information Jose had, they dismounted their horses, bid him farewell, and walked the rest of the road into the scattering of buildings. Strong kept his rifle hidden beneath his canvas jacket to avoid suspicion. With Cate and Mack waiting behind the hostel, Strong lowered his hat and entered the front door. Inside, he didn't see any of Stronovich's enforcers, so he walked up to the desk and asked for a room. The desk clerk assigned him Room #5 (of the ten total rooms in the whole hostel) and gave him the key. Strong asked him about a back entrance, and the clerk pointed him in the right direction.

Around back, the trio ascended the back stairwell and entered Room #5. Inside, they found a creaky bed and a desk. There were no paintings on the wall, no sign of a lamp ever being present, and old wooden floors. Strong pulled out his rifle and leaned it against the wall near the door. Mack took a seat on the bed and sighed. Cate set her document bag on the desk and pulled out the tome from the library and the cipher page. Just as Strong began to walk to the window, someone knocked on the door.

Everyone quickly looked at the door, half expecting it to be riddled with bullet holes at any moment. Strong slowly walked toward the door, moving to the side just in case it was busted down. He reached out and grabbed his rifle that was leaning against the wall. He raised it to his hip and pointed it at the door.

"Who's there?" Asked Strong in a stern voice.

"Ms. Anne Nill," said the voice from the other side of the door.

Cate ran past Strong and opened the door, as if she recognized the name. In walked a small woman dressed in a blue skirt and jacket. Her black bangs were swept to the right and she had two small buns on either side of her head. She wore round black-framed glasses, with "Kelley and Co., London" branded on the side in gold. She kept a stern look on her face. She carried a plaid carpet bag and, on entering the room, set it on the floor.

"Who the hell are you?" Strong lowered his rifle.

"Strong, Mack, this is Ms. Anne Nill," said Cate. "She is a specialist in old books and is—was—Willy's secretary."

After letting Ms. Nill take a seat at the desk across the room, Mack asked her what she was doing there.

"Mr. Voynich was my boss for many years," Ms. Nill explained. "I've been with him since his shop was in England. He was my friend. When I saw what happened to him in the papers, I tracked you all down and followed you here."

"I can't believe it, Anne," Cate smiled. "You are more resourceful than I ever knew."

"Mr. Voynich and I ran from Stronovich for many years. It's only right that I see it to the end with you three." Ms. Nill never changed her expression, only shifting her head and eyes to match the person she spoke to.

"I have arranged a guide to the crater tomorrow for us," she announced. "Is that suitable?"

"Yes, thank you," Strong replied. "We need to beat Stronovich to the crater."

"We will, Mr. Strong," said Ms. Nill, "We leave at sunrise."

After speaking about the manuscript and exchanging adventure stories for the rest of the evening, the four found some time to rest before their sunrise jaunt to the crater. Cate joined Ms. Nill in her room, while Mack and Strong reluctantly shared the bed in theirs.

Just before sunrise, a chicken outside the hostel woke Strong up. He walked to the window and opened it to let in the fresh mountain air. As he looked out, he could barely make out the street below with the fog that had rolled into the small gathering of buildings. It could hardly be considered a town. Below, he saw a woman lurking in the shadows, hiding herself from the sunlight. He recognized the woman as Ms. Nill.

Putting on his clothes and grabbing his rifle, he snuck out the back door and ran down the back stairwell to follow her. As he plunged into the fog, he thought he lost her. In the fog, it was hard to see anything farther than ten feet ahead of him. As Strong turned his head, he caught a glimpse of Ms. Nill as she glided past a ray of sunlight that showed through two buildings. He gave chase, following her down a side alleyway between a stable and a corn crib. As she disappeared into a small building, Strong slowly crept to it.

Strong followed the side of the shack and came upon a window. When he looked inside, he couldn't see anything past the curtains. Following the building around the back side, he stopped when he saw one of Stronovich's enforcers standing on the back porch, smoking a cigarette.

The man grunted and spit, then threw his cigarette and walked back inside the building. Strong wondered why Ms. Nill had snuck into one of Stronovich's buildings. At first, he feared for her safety, thinking she had unknowingly entered the building when looking for a bathroom or something. Then, another thought entered his mind, one more sinister. Could Ms. Nill be working with Stronovich? After all, she knew of him and, with her boss dead, she might need the money Stronovich could offer her. His mind full of suspicion, Strong disappeared into the fog and returned to the room. Back inside, Mack was putting on his clothes.

"Where have you been, Harvey? Sun's almost up and we gotta meet our transport."

"Sorry, I had to shit." Strong decided to keep his newfound intelligence to himself before he knew the whole truth.

Ten minutes later, Cate burst through the door and shouted, "You won't believe it, Harvey! We have the manuscript!"

"What?" Mack turned toward her.

"How did you get it?" Asked Strong.

Cate gestured toward Ms. Nill, who stood behind her. Ms. Nill gave a faint smirk at Strong.

Cate continued, "Anne snuck out and got it from one of Stronovich's guard shacks on the edge of town. Can you believe it? I thought she was insane for trying such a thing."

Strong tried not to let on that he had already seen Ms. Nill, but he suspected she knew, somehow. Something about her stare made him think she was a woman who knew much more than she ever let on.

"Yeah, insane," Strong admitted. "What were you thinking?"

"Ms. Cate showed me her cipher last evening. Without the manuscript, it is useless. The text in the manuscript could contain important information for our journey. I knew we needed it, so I got it. I can be very silent, so I slipped in and snagged it."

As Nill and Cate opened the manuscript and used the cipher to translate its text, Strong sat on the bed, thinking about Ms. Nill and her true intentions. Mack smoked a cigarette and blew the smoke out the window for the ladies. Soon, Cate had a few sentences translated.

"It talks about a city in the mountains, pre-dating the Incas and the Spanish," she reported. "An archaeologist's dream."

Cate used the cipher to translate a bit more and soon Strong noticed the sun rising behind the building across the street.

"Stronovich is gonna be up soon, I bet," Strong said, "He's gonna check on that manuscript. We gotta get going."

Cate and Ms. Nill ciphered a few more pages and then decided they could do the rest on the road. As Ms. Nill and Mack exited the room, Cate turned to page 34 and ripped it out. She tucked it in her jacket pocket and followed Strong out of the room.

The four snuck to the stable and met Jorge, their guide, to the crater. Jorge had a small wagon pulled by two mules. They piled in the back and Jorge whipped the mules to life. Mack and Strong kept their guns close and their eyes on the road behind them and ahead. Cate and Ms. Nill translated page after page, revealing new information about this lost city.

"This *is* Bacon!" Shouted Cate to Mack and Strong, "He speaks of travelling to South America in search of alchemist's secrets in 1245. He says he followed the trail of gold to the basin and found the city of Quilotoa, made entirely of gold and precious gems mined from the mountains. A true El Dorado!"

"I can't wait," Mack grinned.

"If there's a city of gold, why haven't we heard of it since the 1200s?" Strong puzzled.

Ms. Nill spoke up, "The volcano erupted a year after Bacon arrived in Qualitoa," she said with a stern, almost disappointed voice.

"The volcano likely killed all the plants and animals that Bacon had recorded in the manuscript," Cate went on. "That's why we have never seen any of them in the wild."

"And the city of gold?" Asked Mack.

"Likely destroyed, along with all of its inhabitants," explained Ms. Nill.

"And Stronovich would have no idea it was destroyed without this cipher," said Strong.

After thirty minutes, they were within walking distance of the crater's edges. The sun was up already and was heating the air. As they dismounted the wagon, Jorge said he would stay until they returned, at least until sunset. He threw them two canteens of water and Cate thanked him.

Walking up the side of the crater's edges was like traversing the sand dunes of Egypt, Strong thought. After about ten minutes of climbing, they made it to the precipice and looked out over the crater. From this height, they could see the entire Quilotoa Crater Lake, shimmering a bright teal in the sunlight. The crater's edges were very high, almost like the sides of a small mountain range. Luckily, the part of the crater they were standing on flattened out and was easy to walk down. They followed a small trail until they came to water's edge. There, they stopped and had a drink of water.

"Well," said Mack, "If there's no city of gold, where's Stronovich?"

"Do you think he came already and left when he didn't find any city?" Cate pondered.

"No," Strong countered. "A man doesn't search out a place for his entire life and give up when he doesn't find it on the first try. If he's here, he'll be looking for days to find any remnant of the place."

The four of them followed the path around to the right of the lake. Strong kept his rifle at the ready, while Cate continued to cipher pages from the manuscript as they walked.

"The text really opens your eyes to the world that once inhabited this region. The people had such unique customs, and the plants and animals seem so foreign to the world we know now. It's a shame they're all gone," said Cate.

They continued to follow the loop around and soon their view of the lake was shrouded by large, jutting rocks that sprung up in the midst of the volcanic eruption. Strong felt a sense of foreboding doom as they rounded a loop and the rock ledge rose steadily toward the clouds. A few small rocks fell from the top.

Cate began reading from the manuscript, "It says here that…"

The sound of numerous guns clicking cut her off. Strong raised his rifle up to the rock ledge where the rocks had fallen from. A Stronovich enforcer stood on the ledge, pointing a Thompson submachine gun down at the four of them. Along the ledge, a group of enforcers stood, pointing guns at them. Upon a quick glance, Strong estimated that there were at least eight or nine men.

Before they could fire or retreat, Stronovich and three enforcers walked out from behind a pass in the rock. Stronovich had shed his black jacket and was wearing a white shirt with suspenders. On his hip hung the Tokarev pistol that had taken Willy's life. Strong wondered what happened to Willy's body that they had left on the street?

"Thank you for joining me, Ms. Newsome. Gentlemen, I appreciate the armed escort," greeted Stronovich.

"How did you know where we were?" Cate closed the manuscript and tucking it under her arm, as if to protect it.

"I've always known where you were, Ms. Newsome. As you may well know, I am a very resourceful man." Stronovich motioned behind Cate.

Ms. Nill stepped forward, snatched the manuscript from Cate's arm, and walked to Stronovich. She turned and held up the manuscript to Stronovich's view, then smiled. It was the first time Strong had seen her smile.

"With very resourceful friends," Strong sneered.

Cate stepped forward, and pleaded. "Anne, how could you? How long have you been in his checkbook?"

"Since the day I met you, Ms. Newsome," said Ms. Nill. "Since the day I met Wilfrid Voynich. My working with him wasn't a matter of chance."

So, Strong figured, Ms. Nill was the secret weapon of Stronovich. Working with Willy, watching his progress, monitoring his whereabouts. With Ms. Nill on the inside, Stronovich could spend his time searching for the other half of his map. An enforcer stepped forward and ordered Mack and Strong to drop their weapons. Against their will and better judgment, they did. Strong stepped closer to Cate to guard her against these tormentors.

Stronovich opened the manuscript and, from his pocket, pulled a piece of parchment. He turned the manuscript to a specific page and laid his piece of parchment onto the page. For a moment, Stronovich tried to used the cipher to decode the text on the page, but became visually frustrated when he couldn't find the answer. He looked up at Cate, walked to her, and stopped in front of her and Strong. Strong remembered the man's immense size now.

"Where is the page?" Asked Stronovich firmly.

"What page?" Cate retorted.

As soon as the words left her mouth, Stronovich's hand struck the side of her face. She fell.

Instantly, Strong jumped at him, but Stronovich pulled his pistol and pointed it at Strong's face. Reluctantly, Strong fell to his knees and lifted Cate to hers. Then, Stronovich pointed the pistol at Cate.

"No!" Shouted Strong, shielding her from the pistol's barrel.

"Give me the page! Page 34! The one with the rest of the map, woman!" Shouted Stronovich.

"I've got it," said Mack, stepping forward.

Stronovich looked up at Mack, then back at Strong and Cate. He turned and looked at Ms. Nill. She shook her head.

"You wouldn't lie to me, would you?" Stronovich pointed his gun at Mack.

"I wouldn't shake your hand with a ten-foot pole," Mack spat into the rock.

Stronovich smiled. He lifted the barrel of his gun and fired over Strong's head. The shot hit Mack in the stomach and he fell to his knees, grabbing at his abdomen. Blood poured out of the bullet hole and ran through Mack's fingers. Strong ran to Mack and grabbed his abdomen to keep the blood from pouring out.

"Stay strong, Harvey, you got to save Cate," Mack said as he fell backward, but Strong caught him.

Stronovich pointed his gun at Cate, saying. "I think you'd better tell me where that page is, or Ms. Newsome will be lying next to your friend."

Strong lifted his head, tears filling his eyes. He looked at Cate. She shook her head "no" and tears filled her eyes, too.

"It's in Cate's jacket," said Strong.

Cate's head fell, disappointed. Stronovich smiled, reached down, and pulled the page from Cate's jacket. Stronovich put his pistol away and walked back to Ms. Nill, who held the manuscript. After placing the page in the manuscript, Stronovich looked up and around at the crater, and then back at the map. He

...Mack... fell to his knees, grabbing his abdomen...

smiled and looked at Ms. Nill. She smiled back.

"You see, Ms. Newsome, with a little luck, and hard work, research can accomplish anything. I've spent my life searching for Quilotoa, and now I am within sight. This map is a route to the city."

"It's gone!" Cate shouted, "The blast destroyed everything within a mile radius."

"Yes, you are right. The blasts destroyed the architecture of the city and many of its inhabitants. Bad luck, really, building a city on top of a volcano. Yet, the artifacts, the stones, the remnants of the city, those were all moved to a secret location during the Spanish inquisition," Stonovich explained.

"You killed Willy for profit? For gold and artifacts? Is that worth a man's life?" Cate screamed.

"Yes. His life was worth it. When I stumbled upon a reading of Bacon's lost years and then, the manuscript, I knew a find like that could make me a man with no equal. For profit, though? No, not for money. The hidden treasures of Quilotoa, the secrets it contains, that is worth the journey I have undertaken."

Stronovich motioned for his men to grab Strong and Cate. Two men grabbed Strong by each arm. Another took hold of Cate. Stronovich ordered the rest of his men somewhere else, but Strong couldn't understand the Russian. As they were ordered to follow, Strong looked back at Mack, who was lying on the rock, still holding his stomach. He wondered if it was the last time he would see his best friend.

Stronovich and Ms. Nill led the way, rounding a corner in the pass and coming upon a large rock outcropping in the side of the crater. Stronovich held up the page and his map and smiled. From behind them, the other enforcers arrived, carrying large wooden crates. They set down three crates and used crowbars to open them. Inside were sticks of red dynamite. Stronovich's men set up the sticks next the rock wall where he had shown them. Stronovich, Cate, Strong, and Ms. Nill stepped back behind a large boulder to shield themselves from the blast.

As the last of the dynamite was placed, gunfire from the ledge above surprised them. Everyone fell for cover and Strong looked up to the ridge to catch a glimpse of the shooter. Mack, with a bloody shirt, was shooting both of his pistols from the ledge. He had dragged himself to the ledge, as the front of his body was covered in dirt. The enforcers began firing their weapons in his direction. With Stronovich distracted, Strong punched him in the side of his head, grabbed Cate by the hand, and made a mad dash for the dynamite. He grabbed a stick and pulled a book of matches from his front shirt pocket. He lit it and threw it at the group of enforcers at the bottom of the ledge. Grabbing Cate's hand again, they made a sprint away from the lit dynamite.

After a moment, the dynamite exploded right in the middle of Stronovich's enforcers. Among flying articles of clothing and shards of rock were pieces of Thompson submachine guns and flesh. The blast of Strong's dynamite set off the other sticks off dynamite and the boom was so loud that Strong and Cate fell to the ground and covered their heads. Rock rained down from above and he pulled Cate beneath him to shield her.

When the booming commenced and the dust settled, they crawled out from under the rock they had taken shelter to assess the scene. No one was present. In fact, a single, whole person was nowhere to be found. The wreckage reminded Strong of battlefields during the war. He looked up on the ledge, remembering Mack and his wound. Mack's head peered up and over for a second and he smiled at Strong.

Strong shouted up at him, "I'm coming up for you, hold on."

"No! A Russian won't take me down. Go get that bastard for me," shouted Mack as he threw Strong's Henry rifle over the ledge.

Strong ran out and managed to catch it before it shattered on the ground. He checked his ammunition and then looked around for Stronovich.

"He's gone inside that large hole in the side of the crater, with that bitch Ms. Nill," shouted Mack.

Strong and Cate ran into the hole after Stronovich and Nill. Inside, they found a small passageway in the rock just big enough to fit a body through. It looked like it had been carved into the crater. It wasn't the work of dynamite. Without speaking or hesitating, Strong and Cate crawled through the passageway and darkness was all they could see in front of them. A moment later, the light behind them began to fade. As they felt their way through the passageway, it soon opened up and they were able to stand. Two corridors split off from one another, with the one on the right ascending vertically into the mountain.

"Look," Cate whispered, pointing at faint light at flickered on the wall.

"If I was Stronovich, I would follow that one. Let's go right," said Strong, and they did.

Up they crawled, until the steps of the stone passageway seemed to turn into vertical stairs. It was like climbing a ladder. After nearly fifteen feet of climbing, the passageway plateaued and they were able to stand. As they walked further down, they realized they were standing on a ledge. The passageway opened in a large cavern inside the crater mountain. Faint light flickered down from above and they realized that a thousand tiny holes on the ceiling allowed sunlight to permeate the cavern. Down below, nearly fifty feet, were thousands of stone sculptures, clay artifacts, and gold jewelry. The cavern looked like a large treasure chest, with all of the valuables of a civilization stuck inside.

"The last remnants of the city of Quilotoa," whispered Cate, her eyes flashing back and forth from object to object. She was amazed, as was Strong. He wasn't even sure he had believed it up until now.

Below, they heard people talking. Strong and Cate dropped their heads at first, but then raised them enough to listen. It was Stronovich and Ms. Nill, who were now speaking in Russian. Strong raised his rifle to end Stronovich's life, but Cate grabbed it and lowered it.

"If you miss, we will lose the element of surprise. They might get away," Cate cautioned.

Strong agreed, so they crawled down to the end of the ledge and found what looked like stairs on the side opposite of where Stronovich was inspecting his prizes. They slowly descended the steps, often losing sight of their targets when a stone pillar would shroud their vision. Soon, they were at the bottom and began to notice the various types of artifacts they were walking amongst.

"These are some of the most unique finds I've ever seen," whispered Cate as she passed the figure of a large man, bearded with wings and pointed ears.

Strong wondered what Mr. Shue would think of these. Strong had abandoned the museum while guarding relics and here he was doing it again in Ecuador. He realized it was time for a career change. Strong told Cate to wait behind a stone statue as he continued on to surprise Stronovich.

Ms. Nill was inspecting a golden idol of a woman while Stronovich rummaged through a box of artifacts. Strong crept up behind a large gilded statue and crouched behind it.

"*Gde knigi sekrety? Gde blagochestivyye zatverdevayet?*" Stronovich asked himself aloud.

Strong raised his rifle and pointed it at Stronovich. He walked out from behind the gilded statue and cocked the lever on his rifle. Suddenly, Stronovich turned and grabbed for his pistol. Strong fired once, hitting Stronovich in the wrist. The pistol fell from his hands and hit the floor. Stronovich groaned in pain, but didn't fall to the ground. He was a large man, and it would take more than one bullet to take him down. Ms. Nill turned to face Strong, still inspecting the golden idol.

"So, it seems you have survived," said Stronovich.

"Seems that way, huh." Strong cocked the lever on his rifle again.

"Ask yourself something: why would you keep this treasure from the world?" Stronovich let his wounded hand fall limp and blood trickled onto the floor.

"I never had a problem showing this to the world. You, however, won't be the one making the speech."

"I will split it with you. Half for me, half for you. This is my only offer," said a smiling Stronovich.

"I don't think you're in any position to be offering deals." Strong motioned to the rifle in his hands.

"Do you really believe you are the only one with a gun in this room?" Stronovich nodded to the area behind Strong.

Strong took the bait and turned to look. Ms. Nill dove for the pistol on the floor, grabbed it, and fired at Strong. Strong dove for cover, while Stronovich ran off into the treasure trove of artifacts. Strong jumped behind the gilded statue as Ms. Nill fired all eight rounds until the pistol clicked empty. Strong turned and pointed the rifle at her. He contemplated shooting her, but his dilemma was nixed when Cate appeared behind Ms. Nill and whacked her in the back of the skull with a rock. Ms. Nill fell to the ground, out cold.

"That's for Willy, you bitch," Cate growled.

Strong grabbed the pistol and threw it into a dark corner.

He turned to Cate. "Stronovich is in here somewhere. Be careful, Cate, I don't want you caught in the crossfire."

"Wait, Harvey. Let me be the distraction. If we make him think he's got me to leverage with, he'll give himself up to you."

"What? And make me try and make a shot with him holding you?"

"No, you won't take the shot," she pointed to his knife. He smiled, pulled the knife from the sheath and handed it to her. She placed it in the back of her belt, pulling her blouse over to cover it from view. She turned to locate Stronovich, but Strong grabbed her arm, pulled her back, and kissed her deeply.

Moments later, Strong was creeping among the artifacts again. As he did, he saw the most odd and fantastical creatures and treasures he had ever seen. It truly was the greatest find the world would have ever known. He watched Cate walk down the center of the room. Moments later, Stronovich appeared from the darkness and hit Cate in the side of the head with his forearm. Strong wanted to attack him, but Cate would have advised him to stay, so he did. Stronovich smiled, grabbed Cate and picked her up.

"I've got your lovely maiden here!" Stronovich shouted out.

Strong stepped out from behind the statues and pointed his rifle at Stronovich, who grabbed Cate in a chokehold.

"It looks like the tables have turned." Stronovich's black beard wiggled with every word.

Strong pointed his rifle, but then dropped it to the floor. He tried to look defeated.

At the moment Stronovich laughed out in victory, Cate reached back and pulled out the knife. She was perfect height to raise her arm and stab the sharp blade right into the front of Stronovich's thigh. He hollered out in pain and grabbed Cate around the neck. She squirmed, but his grip was too tight. Just as Strong lunged for his rifle, Stronovich chucked Cate nearly five feet, she crashed into Strong and they toppled to the ground. Stronovich picked up the rifle, pointed it, and fired. The shot took off the head of the statue behind Strong and Cate. Strong grabbed Cate and threw her over his shoulder. He ran away from Stronovich and the rifle, weaving in and out of the artifacts to avoid taking a bullet.

The wild shots from Stronovich were puncturing the walls of the room. Water seeped in from their gashes and poured down to the floor. Strong turned to look for Stronovich, but he wasn't firing. Setting Cate down safely behind a large wooden crate, Strong crept around the edge of the room to find Stronovich. He passed a large, emerald figure of a winged creature and then walked through an "alley" of pottery. He ended up on a small clearing in the treasure room and cautiously looked around, but didn't see any movement in the shadows. Out of the corner of his ear, he heard the water pouring down the walls.

In a split second, Stronovich was upon him from behind. He grabbed Strong around the waist and flipped him backwards. He fell to the floor with a thud. Stronovich ripped his own shirt off and revealed a muscular torso covered in tattoos. The tattoos looked like ancient writings and illustrations. Stronovich kicked Strong in the gut and he fell onto his back. Stronovich shoved his boot into Strong's neck. He pressed down harder and harder. Strong tried to pry the boot free from his neck, but Stronovich's weight was immense.

"Now you will know pain, Mr. Strong," snarled Stronovich.

Stronovich lifted Strong front the ground and tossed him like a ragdoll across the clearing. Strong hit a stone statue and fell onto the floor with a thud. Strong felt the blood gush from his mouth and nose, and his ribs ached. He grabbed for his knife, but it was still stuck in Stronovich's leg.

As Strong slowly raised himself from the floor, Stronovich was upon him again. Stronovich grabbed him in a chokehold and lifted him above his head. Strong felt the life leaving his body and all he could do was balance himself by grabbing Stronovich's arms. Just as Strong began to black out from loss of air, a shot rang out.

Stronovich wobbled and coughed up dark red blood. He lost his grip and Strong fell to the floor. On his knees, he saw the knife sticking out of Stronovich's leg. Strong grabbed the knife, pried it out, and, with all his might, ran the knife up and through the underside of Stronovich's head. Stronovich wobbled backward with a few steps and fell dead.

Strong saw Cate holding the Henry rifle, smoke pouring out of the barrel. At that moment, the far wall of the room busted open and a large river of water began pouring into the room. Statues and gold idols were submerged and water quickly reached Strong's feet. He willed himself up and pulled the knife from Stronovich's head. He wiped the blood on Stronovich's black pants and then sheathed the blade. He grabbed the rifle from Cate and threw it around his back by the sling. Cate grabbed his hand and they ran toward the exit passageway.

"We gotta get outta here before the place is flooded!"

"I'm right behind you," Cate shouted.

As they ran, they watched the last bits of treasure and artifacts pass them by. Strong thought of reaching out his hand and grabbing a handful, but curses haunted his mind. He knew some things were not meant to be found. Cate was running behind him steadily, but then dropped back. Strong stopped and searched for her in the darkness, finally seeing her where they had first encountered Ms. Nill and Stronovich. The manuscript was lying on the ground. Cate grabbed it and began to run toward Strong.

"C'mon, Cate, we gotta get out," he shouted.

As Cate ran, Ms. Nill sprang upon her, knocking the manuscript from her hands with a large piece of wood. Cate and Ms. Nill battled for the manuscript, pulling on each other's hair and arms. Nill grabbed Cate and they began tussling on the ground. Strong ran to them, pulled out his rifle, and whacked Ms. Nill across the back. She fell on the manuscript. Cate tried to pry it out, but Strong grabbed her and pulled her away.

"Leave it! It's not worth another life."

Cate tried to free herself from his grip, shouting, "No! I can't leave it."

Strong turned her and looked in her eyes, saying, "I can't leave here without you, Cate. I need you in my life. You make it worth living."

She stared into his eyes. She looked back at Ms. Nill and the manuscript. After a second, she shook her head and they ran toward the exit. Just then, a large piece of the ceiling fell in front of them and they had to redirect their route. Then another piece fell. Water poured in from the sides and from the ceiling. The room filled up a foot high in mere seconds. As they reached the passageway, they found it submerged in four feet of water and rising.

"We'll drown if we go in there," Cate looked afraid.

Strong looked around, trying to figure out a solution. He contemplated busting through the wall to try and escape, but that idea quickly left his mind. After a moment, he remembered the stairway and the ledge that led to the upper passageway.

"Remember how we came in? That's our way out!" Strong shouted over the rumble of the water pouring in and the ceiling collapsing.

They ran as fast as they could through the rising water, sloshing their feet through piles of pottery and coins. As the water was nearly waist deep, it took a fair amount of time and effort before they made it to the stairwell. Strong lifted Cate out of the water and set her on the vertical stairwell, then climbed after her.

They made it to the ledge just as half of the ceiling gave out and fell in, destroying the treasures beneath it. They sprinted down the ledge, finally seeing the opening in the passageway too late. Strong remembered there was a vertical drop in the passageway. He slipped and tried to slow down, but skidded into the hole and fell nearly fifteen feet into the darkness.

Strong hit the sides of the passageway on the way down, injuring his left shoulder and receiving numerous scrapes and bruises. At the bottom, he fell into a deep pool of water. A moment later, Cate fell in beside him. They surfaced and found each other in the darkness. Strong felt the rifle on his back, bobbing up and down in the water. They swam toward where they knew the exit to be, using their hands to find their way. After a moment, and some brief moments of terror and confusion, Strong found the opening with his feet and they dove under.

Strong saw nothing but black. The water around him muffled all sound and made his nerves stand on edge. He felt as if he were in a womb, but one that smothered and killed. He feared he, or Cate, would never reach the other side and would die in this place. He found slight comfort in their dying together, but not much. Just as he began to squirm from the sheer terror of the thought of death, he poured out of the opening in the side of the crater and fell onto the hot rocks outside.

He opened his eyes and saw the sunlight beaming down on him. By now, it was high in the sky. He lifted his head and looked around. Cate was lying five feet from him on her side. She wasn't breathing. He lifted his sore body and crawled to her. He flipped her over and began pushing on her chest. He breathed life into her mouth and, for a moment, thought she was dead. Suddenly, she coughed water up out of her lungs and breathed in the warm air. He grabbed her and hugged her tightly, kissing her face and lips. He never wanted to let her go again.

After they sat in the hot sun for about an hour, Jorge arrived with the wagon and a half-dozen other villagers to help. He spoke Spanish to them the entire time they were loaded into the wagon, but Strong couldn't understand him. Strong was laid beside Cate in the wagon, who was silent but alive.

"Wait—Mack—my friend," shouted Strong, trying to jump from the wagon. He imagined Mack had bled out on that ledge, alone. Jorge and two other men grabbed him and said something to him in Spanish. He couldn't understand them.

Jorge grabbed the sides of Strong's face and slowly said to him, "*Su amigo, Mack, está en el pueblo. Él está vivo. Él está bien.*"

Strong suspected Jorge understood what he asked, and Jorge was trying to respond. Strong had not the will to argue any longer. He shook his head and fell back in the wagon.

When he awoke, Strong was in the hostel. The daylight poured in and hit him in the face. He realized he was lying on the bed. Cate was next to him. Jorge walked in and said something in Spanish again. Strong didn't know what day it was or how long they had been out, but he wanted to see Mack again. Jorge helped him out of bed and a small woman came into the room. She had fresh bandages and began tending to Cate. Satisfied Cate was well-attended, Strong followed Jorge into the room next door.

When he walked in, he saw a man lying in bed, bandages around his waist. He recognized the bald head and goatee. It was Mack. Strong ran to the bed and sat down, grabbing Mack's hand. He smiled.

"Mack—thank God, thank God." Mack opened his eyes slowly.

"Harvey. I'm glad to see you."

Over the next hour, they exchanged stories of what happened inside and outside the treasure room. Mack relayed to Strong that Jorge had arrived with the wagon and his men soon after the explosion. They loaded him up and took him to town for medical care.

Strong returned to Cate's room, finding her awake and smiling. They hugged and kissed each other for hours, happy to be alive and together.

Later, once Cate was able to converse with Jorge, they learned that anyone within ten miles heard the blast. Jorge told the townspeople that Strong, Mack, and Cate had stopped a team of Russian miners from digging up the Crater in search of gold. Everyone was pleased with them took good care of them until they healed up.

Three weeks later, Mack was well-enough to travel, so they said goodbye to their new Ecuadorian family, bought three plane tickets, and headed back to New York.

Mack made *Ricardo's* his first stop when he got home, telling all the guys all about their adventure. He never left out any detail, but no one totally believed him anyway, so Strong didn't feel the need to stop him. After a lost manuscript, a maniacal Russian, and a trip to Ecuador brought them back together, Strong and Cate decided it was meant to be. She cleaned out her office and ended the lease. Deciding it was closer to their friends, Cate moved out of her apartment and into Strong's. She told him to quit his job at the museum if he hated it so much, but Strong protested.

"That job brought Willy to me—and me to you," Strong argued. Cate was pleased and kissed him passionately.

Some months later, they received a package from Ecuador. It was heavily glued and covered in stamps and postal marks. It was from Jorge. Inside, it had a letter, thanking them again for their help and asking them to write them often from America. Inside, it had Cate's glasses that one of Jorge's men had found in the jungle around the crater. When Strong read that part of the letter, Cate picked up the glasses and looked at them. They were round and black-framed. On the side, they were branded "Kelley and Co., London."

THE END

THE JOURNEY THROUGH
THE VINLAND VEIL

Austria, 1933

Walking through the row of large oak trees reminded Harvey Strong of the forests of Belgium that he traversed during the Great War. He remembered the hard wood and gleaming steel of the rifle in his hands, the consistent and deep panting of each man as they sprinted through the forest like a herd of frightened deer, and the sound of mortar rounds blasting away the world around them. It was a warzone. Stella Matuntina was anything but a warzone. The picturesque vista that the Jesuit Catholic college sat within was surrounded by rolling tips of cradling mountains. One rather large, jutting crest seemed to lean out and over the school, as if guarding it from some ethereal evil. Stella Matuntina had operated uninterrupted for almost 300 years, interrupted only for a papal decree and the onset of the Great War. That damned war seemed to stop everything, thought Strong. He kicked a small acorn from the sidewalk path that he was walking down. As he passed one of the classroom buildings, he caught his reflection in the plate-glass window. Even in the moonlight, he could see himself clear enough.

He looked oddly out of place. In his gray wool suit, he looked more like a bear in costume. His memories jumped to adventures, of dusty, dirty clothes, and guns blaring. It had already been nearly three years since he and Cate were married. He sighed at the thought of marriage. Love was a fine thing indeed, but not something that stuck to him well.

Cate's work had brought them first to Berlin last year, and now to Feldkirch. She was working on decoding a 15th century text in some form of ancient German script. Strong didn't find her work interesting, but the change of scenery it offered was worthwhile. Two years prior they had visited Asia, then a quick jaunt in Peru, followed by a stay in Brazil. As one of the leading philologists in America, Cate's services were needed the world around.

Earlier in the evening, Cate had managed to find time to eat dinner with Strong. After scarfing down her quail and potatoes, she was back to work trying to meet the deadline of a local museum. The museum work helped fund the school's programs. After that, Strong decided he'd go for a walk instead of looking at the same newspaper again. He couldn't even read German, so he wasn't quite sure what the news was.

Rounding a bend in the path, he passed a young man in priestly robes. The men exchanged a "hello" and continued on their separate paths. Everything here with a job was involved in the Church in some way. Most of the well-to-do Catholics sent their best and brightest to be taught theology, law, and natural sciences from the priest/scholars. Strong laughed at the notion. He remembered the "nuns" that had educated him at the boys' home, Mother of Mercy, in Brooklyn. He didn't recall much teaching. Mostly chidings and a few beatings.

As Strong pulled his hand from his pocket and took his pipe to his mouth, he was struck in the front by an older gentleman. Strong's pipe fell from his hands, but his large body did not budge. The old man fell to his rear and a leather satchel landed on the ground next to him. Strong went to reach for the satchel to help the old man up, but the gentleman snatched it first and let out a German curse.

"Excuse me, padre," Strong grabbed his pipe and dusted it off.

"*Ich habe keine Zeit, um mit Ihnen zu schuften bekam,*" said the old man. He looked at least seventy years old. His glasses were fogged up from heavy breathing and he wore a black suit. His eyes were bright blue.

Strong thought him to be a priest. Likely fetching some lost prayer or misplaced rosary. Strong started walking past the old man, content to continue his evening alone. He heard the rustle of the old man's ascent to his feet and departure toward the school entrance. Blowing a piece of dust from the stem of his pipe, Strong stuck the reed back in his mouth.

As he looked up, a group of four men assembled in a compact unit were marching past him. Strong stepped to the side and into the grass to avoid being run over. He noticed a shining swastika on the shoulder of the closest man. Each wore gray, starched uniforms. Mostly, Strong stared down at the pistols on their hips.

The group of men high-stepped past Strong, not even pausing to assess his presence. Strong watched the group follow the sidewalk down toward the entrance, where the old man had been. He noticed the four men disappear down the alleyway between two buildings and into the darkness. Strong hesitated for a moment, but then turned back toward his destination.

Instantly, he heard the crash of something—body against brick, possibly—and turned back around. He pulled his pipe from his mouth and placed it inside his jacket pocket. He heard the shout of someone in German and the swift motion of a fist through the air. He had heard such movements a thousand times, but only now did he realize the true nature of the Nazi presence.

Strong ran down the sidewalk toward the alleyway and turned the corner. Two Nazis were holding the old German man down on the ground. He was bleeding from his mouth. The other two were speaking in German. One turned around and saw Strong, but did not think him a threat.

Strong hesitated. Sure, he was a good man who would help those in need. Yet, the rise of the Nazi regime, especially in this part of the world, was unquestioned. He might be getting more than he bargained for tonight. Either way, he thought, he was going to do what was right. Even as a child, it was his purpose, his calling.

Strong walked up behind the nearest Nazi and placed a well-timed fist into the back of his skull. The younger man fell to the ground, crushing his hat on the pavement. He was out cold. The other Nazi shouted at Strong and went for his pistol. Strong smirked and kicked the Nazi's hand away from the holster. He laid a right fist into the Nazi's jaw and followed it with a left to put him on his back.

Another man jumped him from behind and put him in a chokehold. Strong backpedaled until the parasite's body slammed against the brick wall of the nearest building. The man slumped to the ground with a groan. Suddenly, Strong was looking down the barrel of a Luger. The fourth Nazi had managed to get the drop on him. He shouted a German order, but Strong did not move. He truly didn't know what was being asked.

From behind the Nazi, the old man rose up from the ground, lifted his briefcase overhead and smacked it across the head of the Nazi. Strong seized his opening and tackled the aggressor to the ground. He walloped him with a few right and left fists until he was unconscious.

"Hurry," said the old man in heavily-accented German, "there are more and we shouldn't be here any longer."

Strong quickly agreed and followed the old man's shadow through the faint moonlight.

Harvey Strong found himself in a candle lit room in the faculty dormitory across campus. The old man had led him to a desk in the corner of the room. Strong stood waiting for something to happen, but nothing did. Once, they heard shouts from outside, and the old man covered the lit candle to conceal their hiding place. After a few minutes of silence, the old man spoke first.

"Thank you," he said, in a faint voice. He seemed almost withering away, as if pieces of him were dying off. The vigor he displayed in the fight was a miracle to Strong.

"No problem, father," said Strong.

"You know me? Even out of my robes?"

"I've seen a priest or two, in my day," Strong walked to the window and peered out, assessing the situation. Nothing appeared. "What was all that about?"

The old man pulled his briefcase open and began searching its contents. Strong watched on, hoping to see some Catholic idol of great importance. Instead, the old man pulled out a small folder and placed it on the desk. He turned to Strong, as if wanting to tell a great secret. Instead, he gave him a warning.

"Mister, whomever you are, whatever you do, I thank you for helping me tonight. You didn't have to do that. Yet, I don't think you want any part of this. Truly."

Strong was taken back by the cautionary tale. Most people flocked to use his strength and experience for their own gain or protection.

"I understand and appreciate that. Truly," Strong picked up his Stetson from the bed where he had dropped it and walked out of the room.

As he walked down the hallway toward the exit, feeling a bit undervalued. He felt empty, as if he had no purpose. Part of him wanted to know what all the excitement was over some Austrian priest and a file folder. Yet, another part of him felt free. For three years, he had traveled with Cate and lived the life he never dreamed he would. Waking up late, eating real meals, and sustaining a marriage. He found himself impressed with... himself.

Strong exited the building and began walking the path back toward Cate's office. He wanted to hold and kiss her, and never tell her anything about what happened with the priest and the Nazis. It was his little treat. His last taste of the sweet thrill of adventure. In a moment's time, he would return to his new life. Unfortunately, standing in his path was a regiment of Nazi soldiers.

Strong ducked behind the nearest tree and tried his best to conceal his person. Had they really brought a whole army... for him? He knew he could hit hard, but he was impressed. Strong glanced around the bark of the tree and watched the regiment. A man in the middle of the bunch, middle-aged and clearly-shaven was barking orders. It seemed they were searching for something. Two soldiers entered the nearest building and began shouting at the sleeping people inside. Upstairs, Strong saw the candlelight flickering in Cate's office. He imagined what they might do to a beautiful, lonely woman.

He prepared to move from his position, but then two detachments of Nazis walked past him and split into the only two directions that were his options for escape. Strong knew he could not get to Cate now. He bowed his head for a moment, defeated.

Then, the screams of a woman broke the silence of the night. Strong turned around and looked into the darkness, and saw Cate. Two Nazis were holding both of her arms and she was struggling to free herself.

"Let go of me!" She shouted. Strong desperately wanted to help her.

"*Diese Frau wurde Inspektion alte Dokumente. Sie könnte mit der Karte beteiligt sein,*" said one of the soldiers.

The commander positioned himself in front of Cate and looked her up and down. He smiled, then said, "*Bitte sagen Sie uns, wo die Karte befindet,* Miss."

Strong knew Cate didn't know German. She made a face at the commander.

"Tell us where the map is, miss?" said the commander in English.

"I don't know about a map." Cate replied.

The commander lost his smile. "Do not test me, woman. I will do what I must to find it."

Strong jumped from his position and revealed himself to the unit. Guns were pointed at him immediately and he raised his empty hands. He was not carrying a gun tonight.

The commander turned to Strong and showed a look of confusion. A soldier spoke up in German.

"Ah," said the commander, "it seems you can't get enough of my soldiers."

"Yep, sure can't. Too bad it takes four of them to have any fun."

The commander smiled, "I like you, sir. However, you're lucky you are not dead right now. Why have you revealed yourself?"

"That's my wife," Strong had to play all of his cards.

"Ah, I see," contemplated the commander, "Well? Where is the map?"

"I don't know about any map," Strong retorted, "and neither does she."

The commander pulled his pistol and pointed it at Cate's head. "Well, that's a problem, because I have this pistol and I would rather have a map instead. Trade?" Strong didn't know of any map in the area. He had to think.

"Here," said a voice from behind Strong.

Strong turned swiftly around saw the old priest standing behind him. The same file folder was in his hands from up in the room.

The commander smirked. He lowered the gun and held out his hand to receive the map. "We meet again, Father Fischer."

The old man slowly walked to the commander, as if defeated. He timidly laid the folder in the hands of the commander, who immediately held it tight between his fingers. He opened the folder and pulled out a small piece of parchment. Strong could not make out anything on the paper.

"So it seems, Colonel Beckert," said the old man, whom Strong now knew as Father Fischer.

Seemingly satisfied, Colonel Beckert put the parchment back in the file folder and re-holstered his pistol. He issued an order and the regiment of Nazi soldiers reformed itself. The two men holding Cate pulled her along with the group.

"Hey," shouted Strong, "what are you doing with my wife?"

Colonel Beckert turned around, smiling. "You seem like a capable man. Whomever you are, I applaud your efforts. Had you been born German under the Third Reich, you would be a valuable asset. Unfortunately, you are not. I cannot have you impeding this mission. A man with something to lose is a muzzled dog. You'll get her back when we are finished."

Strong started walking toward the Colonel, but Father Fischer stopped him. Strong protested, but Father Fischer put his hand on Strong's shoulder.

"Colonel Beckert would not hesitate to kill you here and now. Then, your wife would have no one."

Strong could not argue the priest's logic. Cate looked back from across the courtyard, with sadness and helplessness in her eyes. He yearned to push past Fischer's hand, shoot Beckert in the chest, and take Cate home. But he could not. It would mean his death and, by relation, Cate's death. He had to follow them and wait for the opportune moment.

"All right, Father, you win," Strong capitulated.

Later that evening, Strong and Fischer agreed to take a car to the Nazi camp outside Dornbirn. They loaded their gear—Strong slapping his pistol on his hip and covering it with his jacket—and departed at first light. Strong was silent as he drove the green Opel Kadett. He wasn't even sure whose car it was, but Fischer had the keys. Strong was focused on retrieving his wife.

"We'll find her," said Fischer, "I know it."

Strong did not respond. He was fuming inside. Cate was his world now and no one, he had thought, would change that. His thoughts strayed to Beckert— his hideous and mocking smirk. He so badly wanted to kill the man. Then he thought of the folder and the parchment.

"What's this map about?" Strong queried while keeping his eyes the lightly lit road ahead of them. The red sun was peeking over the surrounding mountains of Feldkirch.

"Ah, yes, the map," Fischer adjusted his round-rimmed glasses and leaned back against the leather seats of the Opel.

"In the mid-1500's, the Norse—or Vikings—discovered the area we call Greenland. Well, legend has it they continued searching westward and discovered America. Parts of it, at least."

"What about Columbus? 1492?" Strong remembered his history lessons as a child.

"True. Columbus did indeed discover America—for the Spanish," said Fischer, "but he was not the first. In the early 1100's, the Norse discovered a land beyond Greenland they called 'Vinland.' Leif Erikson is one of the men who made the journey and plotted the course. Legend continues that they made settlements in the southern part of Canada and northeast United States."

"What happened? Why don't we live in New Norway now?"

"We don't know. The settlements eventually died out and the legend continued orally through the years. Eventually, the Catholic Church got wind and created a map from the oral histories. That's the map that Beckert has obtained."

"Why did the Vikings hide it in the first place? Why not announce their discovery to the world?"

"Because they must have found something there worth hiding." Fischer guessed.

"And that's what Beckert is hoping for?"

"Exactly. Beckert was adopted into the Nazi SS by Hitler himself. Beckert was a scholar and treasure hunter before rise of the Third Reich. *Der Führer* seeks what this map is said to lead to."

"Which is?"

"Well, I'm not exactly sure. On the back of the map is an inscription in very faint ink. It's almost impossible to an untrained eye. It says: *Cross the Northern Sea, to the land of the Narrow River. Seek the Holy reward—watch no man groan in pain—by stepping, feet-first, through the eternal veil. Douse thyself in glossy oil, and see thy suffering end.*"

Strong thought to himself. *Riddles, maps, Hitler's army. This was some sort of conspiracy right out of the dime novels.* Then again, his life was something out of a dime novel. Any disbelief he had was quickly stifled. Whether or not it was real, he didn't care. He wanted Cate back. He would do anything to find her.

"All right, so what do we do when we reach their camp?" Asked Strong.

"I'm afraid we might find it empty—of the contents we seek, at least."

"What? What do you mean?"

"The Nazis have an airfield just west of Dornbirn. If they made it there before us, I'm sure Beckert and his team would be on a plane within minutes," Father Fischer looked disappointed in himself.

"So they're long gone? Where to?"

"The map leads to Greenland and the lands to the west. If I was Beckert I might pinpoint my search to the larger cities in those areas."

"Work with me here, Father."

"Uh," said Fischer, thinking aloud, "I'd say Quebec, maybe?"

"All right, where's the nearest airfield that can get us there?"

"Nowhere here, my boy. We could get to London, maybe. Beyond that, we'd need quite a bit of money to make the trip to Quebec."

Strong thought for a moment. Then, getting a new idea, he smiled.

"Father, if you can get us to London, I can get us help and a ticket to Quebec."

After reaching Dornbirn and finding food, Strong and Father Fischer headed west to St. Gallen and chartered a flight to London. With layovers and transfers in Strasbourg, Reims, and Calais, they found it was nearly noon the next day before their plane landed in London. Father Fischer seemed exhausted from the extensive travel, but Strong felt himself getting closer to Cate. It gave him renewed energy.

Bypassing lunch, Strong and Fischer grabbed their bags and headed for the *Galloping Mare*, a pub downtown where Strong had arranged to meet their confidant. As they entered, Strong pulled Father Fischer out of the way of two drunks fighting through the pub. They fell over and through a table near the door and then agreed to return to their drinking. Fischer was obviously out of his element, but Strong smiled. He dropped his bags near the entrance and walked up to the bar. He noticed a burly man hunched over the bar, a large glass of beer in his hands. He walked up behind him and grabbed him around the chest. The man quickly turned, as if to defend himself from an attacker. The Englishman's goatee creased into a smile and he grabbed Strong in a bearhug.

"Good to see you, Mack," said Strong. It had been nearly two years since Mack Thatcher returned home to England. His ex-wife had caught fever and died, so he put in his hand to raise his daughter Ellen.

"You old bastard," said Mack, still smiling, "you look slow."

Strong laughed off the insult in favor of expediting the greeting. He took Mack aside to a corner table in the pub. After an introduction, Fischer joined them and Strong relayed the tale to Mack of Cate's kidnapping. Mack instantly agreed to accompany them on the trip, but Strong protested, bringing up the situation with his daughter Ellen.

"Ah, Ellen," said Mack, "the girl is fiery, I'll give her that. She's staying with her aunt at the moment because she said I'm stubborn and unfit to parent."

Strong smirked, but Father Fischer did not. Strong protested, but Mack, like Ellen has said, was stubborn as hell. Strong gave up his protest and Mack made his plans to accompany them from London to Quebec. Late that day, once Mack picked up his gear and the tickets, they departed London and made their journey over the Atlantic.

Some hours later, the trio arrived in Quebec. Walking through town, they were surprised at the amount of pedestrians, automobiles, and trolleys winding their way throughout the city. It seemed Father Fischer couldn't help

"You old bastard, you look slow."

running into every other person. Strong and Mack walked side-by-side and most people moved out of their way. They soon found a cafe that served beer and stopped for rest and food. After eating, Strong took a hard look at Father Fischer in the daylight. He was definitely over seventy years old. Maybe even eighty. He wondered why a old man was invested in such a crazy scheme.

"Why does this map matter to you so much?" asked Strong.

Father Fischer turned to him and thought for a moment. Then said, "Well, Mr. Strong, after the map was made known to those within the Church, his Holiness created a small group of people tasked with protecting the secret. They didn't know what the map led to, only that it could not be found by the wrong people. I am the descendants of that first group. It was my job to protect the map and I lost it. This is my chance for redemption."

Mack interrupted, "Where do we go from here? Without the map, aren't we shooting at fish in a pond?"

"Actually," Fischer pulled something from his pocket, "we do have a copy of the map."

Fischer pulled out the piece of paper and revealed a roughly-sketched copy of the map. It showed the known world in the mid-16th century: Europe, Africa, Asia, etc. On the far left, in tiny detail, was Greenland and what looked to be some land mass to the west. It was labeled 'Vinland.' Some inscriptions in German accompanied the drawing.

"How do you expect to know where to go if it just shows an outline of Canada?" Mack queried.

"Well," said Father Fischer, "on the back is a faint inscription. I told Mr. Strong about it earlier. It is the secret to continuing the journey from here. I suspect Colonel Beckert had already de-coded that inscription. Luckily, you have me. I have, as well. When it says, '*Cross the Northern Sea, to the land of the Narrow River,*' well, that is the Atlantic and the Narrow River must be the St. Lawrence."

"Okay, so we're in the right place," said Strong. "What's next?"

"'*Seek the Holy reward—watch no man groan in pain—By stepping, feet-first, through the eternal veil,*'" recounted the priest.

Mack thought for a moment. "Holy reward? What's that? God's grace?"

"I don't know," Fischer admitted. "But 'watch no man groan in pain' could be some sort of freedom from the bodily world. Maybe an ascent to the kingdom of God."

Strong had kept silent the majority of the time. He thought about Cate's face, the last time he saw her. He wondered if she knew he was looking for her. Surely, she did.

"Wait," Strong urged. "Listen. The important part is not about what you get. We just need to know where to go. The next line, what was it? 'Eternal veil'?"

"By stepping, feet-first, through the eternal veil," Fischer repeated.

"A veil could be something that covers something, like a forest or a mist or something," suggested Mack.

"Or a mountain range. Where are the mountain ranges here?" Fischer inquired.

"No," Strong replied, "it says 'eternal' veil. Mountains, forests, those all come and go. What is something that is eternal? Maybe representing God or life?"

"Water," Father Fischer blurted. "Water is eternal and represents the cleansing of the soul."

"A waterfall is like a veil. I'm sure there are some falls in these woods," added Mack.

"Good work, men," Strong smiled.

After scarfing down the last of the food and drink, the three men grabbed their gear and went to the nearest library. They inquired about waterfalls in the area. The young lady at the front desk, whose hair was bright red and her blue eyes were a marvel to see, gave them quite a few names.

"Any that really stand out of those?" Strong leaned closer to the girl, waiting for her response.

"Montmorency Falls is the biggest and grandest of all the falls around here. It's really a tourist attraction now, but it sure is grand," she said with a smile.

"Thank you, where is it located?"

The librarian showed him on a map. "But you can't go there right now. It's closed for the next month or so."

"What, why?"

"A team of scientists are looking for Native burial grounds up there," said the girl.

"From where?" Strong inquired.

"Germany."

With the newfound knowledge of the German "scientists" at Montmorency Falls, the trio decided it was best to head up there, as well. Mack brought up that the Nazis probably had most roads up to the falls blocked from public access, not to mention any access from the St. Lawrence River. In need of another method of transportation, they charted a small puddle-jumper plane to take them as close as possible to the falls. Their pilot, Remy, said he would fly them over the falls first and then drop them off in a glen nearby.

As they left behind their least-necessary gear, Strong and Mack began sliding their holsters onto their belts.

Father Fischer spoke up, "I don't think you'll need those, gentlemen. She looks harmless."

Strong and Mack looked at each other, confused.

"What are you talking about, Father?" Asked Strong.

"The girl who has been trailing us since we landed."

Fischer pointed to the back corner of the travel office. Sure enough, the head of a person pulled back with a quick motion. Strong motioned for Mack to go around the other side of the building to flank whomever it was following them. Father Fischer waited near the plane.

Nearing the corner of the building, Strong placed his right hand on the butt of his pistol. He crept slowly until he worked up the courage to stick his neck around the edge of the brick building. Suddenly, a fist connected with his face and he stumbled backwards. A swift kick landed between his legs and he fell to his knees. Strong groaned in pain. Before he could reach for his gun, Mack appeared behind the attacker and grabbed him from behind. The attacker kicked and tried to shove Mack off, but he was too strong.

Strong rose to his feet and looked at the attacker. Whoever it was, *she* was slight and skinny. She wore old, baggy clothes and had a shemagh covering her face. Strong walked up and pulled the shemagh off. Mack let go and his eyes opened wide.

"Ellen!" Mack said, inflecting his voice in surprise. "What are you doing here?"

Ellen Thatcher reached down and picked up her shemagh. She did not look impressed with Strong nor happy to see her father. She had auburn hair, like Mack, but her green eyes were bright and boasted an adventurous streak. She turned to look at Mack.

"Do you think I was going to let you leave me for another ten years while I stay in 'jolly ole' England?" Ellen said sarcastically.

"You were supposed to stay with your Aunt Polly. Does she even know where you are?" Mack's arms were waving in protest.

"Aunt Polly? Know where I am? She doesn't even know which end of the bottle she's drinking out of, sometimes," countered Ellen.

"You're going home right now. Men, I will return in an hour once she's on a plane back to London," said Mack. Father Fischer had walked up after the commotion ended.

"Hell no!" Shouted Ellen as she crossed her arms and glared at Mack.

"Ellen, you're twenty years old. You need to be in school or something, not out here with us tramping around in the bush," her father argued.

"I can fight, I can track, I can survive on my own. The least you can do is let me get to know you a bit before the drink takes you like mom."

Mack began to respond, but stopped. Ellen had hit low and deep. He had no response. He picked up his hat, dusted it off, and put it on his head.

"If you're coming with us, at least keep quiet," Mack said.

Strong was still bent over as Mack walked by him. "She kneed me in the nuts."

"Get used to it," Mack chuckled.

Five minutes later and Remy had the puddle-jumper ready to go for their flight up to Montmorency Falls. Strong and Mack, guns at the ready and hats firmly on their heads, took the front seats closest to the windows. Father Fischer and Ellen sat behind them and waited to be called upon. Remy fired up the plane and took off down the runway. He hollered, "Hold on!" and then the plane was airborne and heading northeast toward the falls.

It was a very quick trip to the falls along the river. After about five minutes, the gigantic falls of Montmorency were in view. White water gushed over the precipice and fell nearly three-hundred feet to a pool of water that contributed to the St. Lawrence further south.

As the plane neared the falls, Strong could make out an encampment at the bottom of the falls with maybe six tents. He judged that a dozen or so men had made the transatlantic flight. What Strong failed to see, and that Remy saw only too late, was a large machine gun set up on the banks at the top of the falls. The engines of the plane weren't hard to miss, and the machine gun let loose a violent spray of bullets that pelted the tiny puddle-jumper. Ten or more holes littered the cabin of the plane and air was sucked out. Ellen screamed and Father Fischer grabbed her arm to comfort her or to comfort himself.

"Dammit, man!" Mack yelled. "They seem to have spotted us first."

Strong nodded his head in agreement as Remy veered the plane away from the falls to save their skin. Unfortunately, the machine gun let out another barrage of lead and, this time, managed to take out the engine of the plane. Black smoke poured into the cabin and choked everyone on board. Before he knew it, Strong couldn't see anything through the smoke or hear a thing over the roar of the failing engine. Suddenly, he felt the air give out from under them and a surge downward. He knew they were falling nose-first into the ground.

From among the commotion, Remy shouted, "Sorry, chaps. I'll do my best to land us square but we're going down for sure."

Strong felt the plane spiral downward until everything went black.

Strong tried to move his legs. Something was holding them down. He tried to open his eyes, but the sunlight overhead blinded him. Slowly, he regained his senses and his ears began to work. It was dead quiet. After a moment, the chirping of a robin flooded his ears and he opened his eyes. Overhead were the branches of maple and oak trees. The sunlight had moved behind one of the canopies and now he could make out their location.

Harvey Strong sat up and assessed the situation. Around him lay the scattered of the puddle-jumper plane. Suddenly, the thought of the lives of the other members of the flight came to him. He tried to jump to his feet again, but remembered the wreckage that prevented his movement. He pushed his strong arms against the metal, but it would not budge.

Strong peered to his left and saw Ellen slowly getting to her feet. She stumbled for a moment and then held herself up with the help of a birch tree.

"Ellen, help me out here." Strong found his own voice raspy and hardly comprehendible.

Ellen slowly walked over to Strong's location and helped him push the metal wreckage to the side. Finally, his legs were relieved the weight of the debris and he moved them just in time for the metal pieces to crash to the ground. He lifted himself to his feet and dusted off. To his right was Mack, who was already up and helping the elderly Father Fischer off the ground. He noticed a large gash on Mack's head.

"Look's like you took quite a fall," Strong noticed.

"Same to you," Mack tried to muster a smirk.

After a moment, they all reconvened at Strong's location. Ellen looked around frantically.

"Where's the pilot?" She asked.

As Strong and Fischer began looking around, Mack spoke up. "Don't bother, men. I found ol' Remy over in the bushes."

Strong and Fischer stopped and held their heads low. Ellen began walking to the spot where Mack had pointed out. Mack grabbed her and held her tight.

"You don't want to see, love," Mack told her. She shook her head after a moment of contemplation.

As the group slowly pooled together what was left of their gear, the storm clouds overhead began swirling in dark pools of gray. Fischer looked up and surveyed them.

"Looks like a bad storm. We need to get to shelter."

"I agree," Mack nodded.

"Sure, but we need to search toward the falls. That's where Cate is," said Strong.

They began walking back toward the direction of the falls. Strong led the way, limping every so often because of the pain that now swelled his legs. Father Fischer followed behind. For a man of his age and constitution, he had survived unscathed. He was silent. Behind him were Mack and Ellen. Ellen had wrapped a bandana around Mack's head gash and walked close behind him most of the way. The rain at first it was only a drizzle, but soon developed into a downright pour. It was as if the heavens were funneling their rage at them.

As he limped along closer and closer to the falls, Strong felt the presence of the supernatural. It reminded him of the events in Egypt nearly six years before. It gave him chills, but it gave him confidence. He had learned in that time to reckon his fears into action. It had saved him quite a few times already. He hoped that it would save Cate, now.

Lightning flashed and the rain continued to pour down like they were beneath the falls of Montmorency. Soon, Ellen and Mack began to get worried the group might perish in this storm. After some coaxing, Strong agreed, and they sought shelter as quickly as possible. It took them a spell, but Father Fischer managed to find the entrance to a cave that was directly north of the falls. From their position, they could hear the roaring of the water as it fell end over end nearly three hundred feet. Strong pulled a lighter from his pocket and lit it.

Immediately, most of the small cave was illuminated. With no grizzlies or wolves present, Strong motioned for the others to join him. Ellen helped Mack take a seat on the cave floor. He held his head in his hands. Ellen collapsed next to him and then scooted herself back against the cave wall. Father Fischer sat across from them and dropped his backpack to the ground. Strong found himself standing in the middle of the cave, holding his lighter and looking around. It was empty, except for a few bats and bugs. He figured this was as good a place as any to wait the storm out.

For a little while, they drank what water they had. Father Fischer prayed with his rosary and then closed his eyes. Mack replaced his soiled bandana for a new one and Strong kicked at dirt.

In the corner, against the wall, Ellen was humming a low tune. At first, her tone was off, but then she adjusted and for a while it made her compatriots sleepy as if in a hypnotic daze. When her song completed, she shuffled to her feet and began to pace. She was getting antsy. She stepped into the darkness of the cave and disappeared with a faint scream.

Strong jumped to his feet and looked around the cave. He had not been watching her, so he did not know where to look. Mack did likewise, but began following the direction of her sudden scream. They searched until Mack nearly fell down into the hole that Ellen had. Strong grabbed Mack's arm and held him up. He lit his lighter and they peered down inside. Below, they could make out Ellen's body. They hollered to her, but she didn't respond.

"I'm going after her." Mack dropped his backpack.

"No," Strong grabbed his friend by the arm. "That gash of yours will pour blood if you strain yourself now. Tie me off and I'll go."

So they did. Mack used a rope he had brought and tied it around his own waist. He then let about fifteen feet loose and tied the other end to Strong's waist. As Mack lowered him into the dark chasm, Strong heard Ellen start to rustle. He yelled to her that he was coming to help. Finally, he reached the bottom and lit his lighter again. On the wall grew patches of grass. He wrapped a bandana around the grass and secured the bundle to his knife with a piece of twine. From his bag, Strong pulled a bottle of gun oil, doused the bundle, and lit the makeshift torch.

Around him, in the lower cavern, everything was illuminated. Suddenly, his eyes closed from the brightness. He was confused at what was causing such an illumination. He slowly opened his eyelids and his jaw dropped at the sight. Around him lay nearly a dozen chests of gold bars, jewelry, and trinkets. He touched one of the chests and coins fell out of its edges. He remembered Ellen and turned to help her to her feet. She was in amazement, too.

"What is all this?" she asked.

"Father Fischer says the Vikings were here for a few hundred years. This must be a forgotten stockpile of their plunder. Let's go."

"And leave all of this gold?"

Strong pulled tension on the rope. "There are more important things."

As Strong prepared the rope for their ascent and called out to Mack, Ellen looked around her. She noticed a large, gilded dagger near her feet. She picked it up and realized it was not a dagger. It had a chain on top and on the end were teeth. It was a key. She placed it around her neck and put it under her blouse. After a moment, she and Strong were being pulled from the cavern.

Back in the main cavern, Mack grabbed his daughter and held her tight. She was shocked to see him display affection to her.

"I thought I lost you."

Ellen wrapped her arms tightly around Mack's stomach.

"Ladies and gentlemen," said Fischer, staring out the mouth of the cave. "It seems our storm has passed."

"Thank God," Strong smiled. "Let's get our stuff together and get the hell out of here."

The crew began their march toward Montmorency Falls. With each step, they could hear the water pouring more loudly. Strong pulled his pistol from its holster and checked the rounds. Ellen and Mack could tell he was on the warpath.

"What's gonna happen?" Ellen made sure only her father heard her.

Mack hesitated, then replied, "I don't know, but it won't be good."

Finally, the group reached the top of the falls and, from a spot behind a thicket of maple, they spotted the machine gun that had taken their plane down. A single soldier sat smoking a cigarette next to it. Father Fischer crouched down next to Strong.

"It's only a single man, we should bypass him and keep moving," said Fischer.

"And let Remy's death go unanswered?" countered Strong.

"I understand how you feel about that. I feel the same. Yet, you may find that it changes you more than you know now," replied Fischer.

"I've killed many men, Father. The majority deserved it. One more won't change anything." Strong motioned to Mack and they both pulled their pistols and prepared to move in on the Nazi.

Mack pulled his other pistol and handed it to Ellen, saying, "I know you can use one of these, but be careful. Use it only for protection."

As Strong and Mack slowly stalked the lone soldier in the clearing, Fischer and Ellen watched on from their spot behind the maple thicket.

Motioning to Mack to go around the other side, Strong readied himself to ambush the man. He remembered Remy's last words, he remembered the men holding Cate, and all he thought about was getting his revenge for what had been done to him. With Mack in position, Strong burst out into the clearing and cocked his pistol.

Suddenly, a group of Nazis appeared from a nearby path down the side of the falls. They all spotted Strong and Mack and pulled their rifles. Strong fired, hitting the young Nazi point blank and killing him instantly. Mack turned swiftly and began firing at the group of five Nazis near the path. The Nazis returned fire and disbursed into the trees to avoid being slaughtered. Strong ducked down behind a tree to save himself.

Mack crept slowly behind some shrubbery until he heard the breathing of a man behind a red oak tree. Mack dove to his left, landed in the dirt behind the tree, and fired twice. The first bullet hit the man's leg and the second ended his life. Mack rolled through his position and took up behind the tree himself.

Meanwhile, Strong was being flanked by two of the Nazis, each carrying a rifle with a bayonet at the end of it. One of the Nazis was crouched down and the butt of his rifle was jutting out from behind the bushes. The other was slower, but more concealed. Strong knew it he had to be quick. He jumped from behind the bushes and fired his pistol, hitting the butt of the rifle that stuck out and knocking it from the Nazis hands. With the one disarmed, he turned to the other and fired one shot into the chest. It hit lungs and the man fell back coughing blood. Strong turned his attention back to the disarmed Nazi and fired twice, hitting him once in the stomach.

Strong looked around the forest landscape, his pistol funneling smoke

"It's only a single man..."

from the barrel. He knew there were two more. He could see Mack positioned behind a red oak tree in the distance. He searched for the gray uniforms among the greens and browns of the woodland. Finally, he caught sight of one. He was crawling on his hands and knees through the bushes along the edge of the clearing. Strong aimed, but realized he was too far away.

Walking along the edge of the clearing, Strong found himself in a better position to take his prey. Soon, he was upon the man and in a good spot to fire. He raised his pistol, took aim, but did not fire. He felt the end of a barrel against his neck. The fifth Nazi had tracked him and now had the advantage. Strong couldn't see Mack anywhere and hoped, maybe, that Ellen could see his predicament.

"Lass die Waffe fallen," said the German.

Strong had a rough idea what he meant. He lowered his pistol, let it hang on the tip of his finger, and then dropped it to the ground. He thought about Cate and what would happen to her.

He wished they had made a child of their own before he left this world. He hoped she would move on and find love elsewhere when he was gone. Strong breathed deeply, taking in the strong, pure air of the woods. As he let out his breath and closed his eyes, the rifle went off and he heard the sound of a bullet piercing flesh.

Strong opened his eyes. Behind him, the Nazi fell dead from a shot to the head. Strong checked his own body for holes, but he was clear and alive. Strong turned his head and saw Ellen standing in the brush. She was holding her father's pistol, but she was not the killer. Further behind her stood Father Fischer. His eyes were wide and his glasses were foggy from heavy breathing. The rifle in his hands was pouring smoke from the barrel. He had saved Strong's life.

Strong retrieved his pistol and the young Nazi on the ground began pleading for his life. Mack crossed through a thicket and arrived on the edge with them. Ellen and Father Fischer did the same.

"Bitte, Gott, hilf mir. Ich will nicht sterben. Ich bin nur ein Soldat," said the Nazi. His hat had fallen off and his brown hair was dripping with sweat.

While he knew the man was just a soldier taking orders, Strong also knew he must die today, or else risk bringing back an entire troop to wipe them out. Strong raised his pistol and prepared to do the deed.

From his right, Father Fischer put his hand on Strong's arm and lowered the gun for him.

"You owe me a life, Harvey. I choose his," declared the priest.

"Father, this man would kill us in a heartbeat."

"The power you hold in your hand also comes with the responsibility of deciding who meets their end with that power. Look at this man. He is no devil. Yes, he is on the wrong side, but no devil," Father Fischer argued passionately.

Strong stared into the Nazi's eyes and tried to register was Fischer was saying. Strong envisioned himself, in full cavalry gear, riding against the German forces at Antwerp. He remembered the guilt he felt taking the lives of young German men whom he had never met and never would. Today, for whatever reason, he decided he would not take another life.

"You win, Father," Strong holstered his pistol.

Father Fischer motioned to the Nazi to run.

"*Gehen! Lauf! Hier nie wieder zurückkommen,*" Fischer directed.

The young Nazi scrambled to his feet and ran as fast as he could in whatever direction the wind took him. As Mack approached Strong, he did not comment on what happened. They both patted each other's shoulder and nodded their heads.

"We're one step closer to Cate," said Strong, "let's take that path down the side of the falls."

At the bottom of the falls, the group did not find what they expected. The Nazi encampment was empty. They searched the tents, but did not find any people. Mack found some ammunition and distributed it to the group. Father Fischer had left his rifle at the top of the falls, and denied the offer of a replacement. Ellen held her father's pistol in her hands. Strong took a German rifle for his own, preferring it over the six shots his pistol offered.

When they made it through the encampment, they all stared up in amazement at the height of the falls. Montmorency fell three hundred feet to a large pool at the bottom. The spray had already soaked their clothes clean through.

"All right, we're here. What now?" Mack scratched his chin.

Father Fischer spoke up. "The inscription on the original map said: "*step, feet-first, through the eternal veil.*"

"Eternal veil is the waterfall," Strong remembered. "So we need to go feet first through it?"

"Seems like it might just spit us back out. That's a lot of water," Mack pointed out.

"No," said Ellen, from the rear of the group, "not through, but behind it. Look!"

Ellen pointed to a small ledge in the side of the mountain that continued winding behind waterfall.

"Think about it: when you cross on a ledge, you have to go feet-first or you're going to lose your balance and fall off," she elaborated.

Mack smiled and patted her back, "That's my girl."

"All right, let's do it," said Strong.

The group, led by Strong, slowly traversed the narrow ledge. As they approached the falls, it became impossible to keep one's eyes open from the amount of mist spraying at them. So, they moved blindly behind the falls on the inches-wide ledge that their feet hardly registered. Slowly, but surely, they noticed the spray begin to lessen and they opened their eyes. The ledge had led them behind the falls and the mountain had opened its mouth into a large cavern. Strong stepped into the cavern and helped the others inside.

"Look, torches." Ellen pointed to a torch that had been secured to the cavern wall by a hammer and nail.

"These Nazis came prepared," said Mack.

"Hitler has no shortage of money or motivation," said Father Fischer, "these men were well-prepared for what they would find."

"Good for us." Strong flicked the flint on his lighter. "Cause I'm out."

The group slowly descended into the cavern behind the falls. Each was weary of what would surprise them in the darkness. As they descended further downward, the light from the entrance torch faded away and again they found themselves walking blindly.

"Can you see?" Ellen directed her words to her father.

"Grab my hand, honey."

Strong slowly moved along the cavern wall to keep from stumbling or falling into a deep, empty chasm. Suddenly, he felt the wall of the cave fade away he turned to assess the situation. From below he saw the faint glint of torchlight. It must be a passageway.

"Guys, over here," he called out. "There's a passageway that'll take us further down."

The group followed him through the passageway. Strong's eyes slowly adjusted to the growing torchlight ahead of him. When they finally reached the torch secured to the wall of the passageway, they stopped suddenly. Father Fischer ran into Strong's back and, had he another fifty pounds on his frame, might have sent Strong over the edge and down into the chasm below.

Strong spoke up. "The passageway ends here. I'm not sure where to go."

Ellen snaked her way through Mack and Fischer to get to the front of the line. There, she knelt down and looked over the edge. She turned her body around to face them and lowered her bottom half over the edge.

"What are you doing!" Mack cried trying to grab her before she fell.

"Calm down, father," Ellen replied. "There's a rope ladder attached to the side."

With that, the group followed Ellen's lead as they lowered themselves down into the chasm below. Strong couldn't tell exactly, but it seemed like they had dropped ten or fifteen feet. Suddenly, Ellen screamed.

"What?" Strong uttered.

'What is it?" Mack echoed.

"Water," Ellen said, lifting her boot from the icy water.

She slowly lowered her entire lower half into the cave water and bobbed on the surface. After a moment, Strong and Mack did the same. Father Fischer stayed on the rope ladder.

"Look around for an opening," Strong ordered, "or a passageway out of here."

"Those Nazi's went somewhere from here," Mack reasoned.

Soon enough, Mack had found the next part of the passageway and lifted himself from the freezing water of the cavern. He helped Ellen out and then heard Father Fischer splash as he dropped into the water.

"Colder than the usual baptismal water, Father?" Mack said as he grabbed Strong's hand and helped him out of the water.

"I would concur with that," Fischer shivered. "Although, if our water was this cold, we might weed out those who are not true of faith."

After a moment, Father Fischer was out of the water, too, and the group continued down the narrow, dark passageway. As they dropped lower into the mountain, it became colder. Strong pulled his lighter out and tried it again, but the flint only sparked. It needed fluid.

As he rounded a curve in the passageway, he noticed that it made an almost complete turnaround in the other direction. That allowed the flood of torchlight to surprise his eyes and the group of Nazis standing on the other side of the opening to go unnoticed at first. German commands were ordered and two men grabbed Strong by the arms before he could raise his rifle and fire. The transition from complete darkness to bright light had momentarily blinded him and the Nazis got the upper hand. Behind him, he heard Mack and Father Fischer taken hostage. They were thrown down against the cavern floor and kept at bay by the barrel tips of German rifles.

As his eyes adjusted, Strong saw two Nazi soldiers who kept guard on the hostages, while four others were filling wooden barrels of water from a stream coming from the side of the cave wall. Colonel Beckert was standing upright, watching his men fill the barrels. At his feet, Cate sat on the floor, her hands tied behind her back. Strong yearned to touch her and comfort her. Beckert looked over at the new hostages and walked in their direction.

"I see you all have managed to use Father Fischer to find your way to us." He said smiling, his perfect white teeth flashing with each word.

Strong spoke up, "You all left enough of a path for a tank to follow you."

"I like your enthusiasm, Mr. Strong," Beckert approved.

Strong was momentarily confused.

"Ah, yes, I know all of you. I've found your wife, Cate, very informative," Beckert explained.

His use of Cate's name made Strong want to tackle him and strangle the life from his Nazi body. Beckert removed his hat and placed it under his arm. He knelt down beside Strong.

"And very beautiful, too," he grinned cruelly.

Strong struggled to get free, but the two guards stepped up and pointed their rifles in his face. He knew he could not help Cate if he were dead.

"So you're planning to take all that back to Hitler?" Father Fischer surmised.

"Of course," Beckert nodded. "The Führer and his elite officers will require quite a large amount of the substance to make sure the Third Reich fulfills its destiny. I, of course, will need a barrel for myself. I'd like to see the 21st century."

Strong and Mack looked at each other in confusion.

"What is he talking about?" Strong looked at the priest. The old man turned to him.

"That water," Fischer nodded in the direction of the leak flowing from the side of the cavern wall, "is the aquae vitae. Water of life. It gives extremely long life to those who drink from it."

"Like a fountain of youth?"

Beckert laughed, "Exactly right, Mr. Strong! *Ach*, you have some brains after all underneath all that excess. The exact inscription reads, '*Douse thyself in glossy oil, and see thy suffering end.*'"

"That's why the Norse hid their discovery of this land," explained Fischer. "As they mined their cavern for precious gems and gold, they stumbled upon the spring. After realizing its potential, they hid it and made sure their enemies would never find such a power."

"Luckily for us, their enemies did," added Beckert. "The Catholic Church, in all its evil power, stole the secrets from the Norse, my ancestors, and created the map we used to find it again. I applaud the power and foresight of the Church, but its failure to use it thus has only proved dumbfounded."

"The Church recognizes its extraordinary power and understands its destructive ability more so than you or some German revolutionary," Fischer retorted.

Beckert slapped Fischer across the face. Blood trickled from the old man's lip. Strong tried to help him, but the guards held him back.

Beckert ordered the old man raised up and brought to the area around the fountain. Strong and Mack could only watch. As Beckert and Fischer neared the fountain, Cate was brought over to Strong and Mack's location. When she saw Strong, she fell into his arms. Strong held her tight, whispering that everything would be all right.

"Are you hurt, Cate?"

"No, but I'm glad to see you, Harvey. Thank God you've come." They kissed and held each other close.

Meanwhile, Beckert showed Fischer the fountain and then revealed a large pool of water that had accumulated over the millennia beneath the fountain.

"There's enough here to last generation upon generation, even if the fountain dried up today," said Beckert.

"Yes, but no man should have such power, Beckert, it's not God's will."

"Why would God create this if not for us to use?"

"The same reason God allows us war, disease, and famine. These are tests. To see who is truly worthy of God's grace." Fischer would not be cowed.

"I've always envied you, Fischer. You knew exactly where this was your whole life. I'm dreamed of this day since I first heard the story."

"Please, don't use this. It's not the right way," Fischer pleaded.

"Don't order me, Fischer. The Church has done enough ordering across the centuries. It's time for a new power to rise in the world.".

"But, Hitler is just..." began Fischer.

In a swift motion, Beckert pulled his Luger from its holster and shot the old man in the gut. The last words of his sentence faded into a gurgle. Father Fischer fell to the ground. Across the cavern, Strong jumped to his feet and tried to run to Fischer. The guards tried to stop him, but Strong was too big for them to keep back. He ran to Father Fischer and tried to stop the bleeding from his abdomen.

Father Fischer mumbled a statement, "Don't... let him... take it."

Strong rose up from the floor and stared at Beckert. He remembered the sacrifice that Fischer made for him, taking a life to save his own. He looked back at Cate and smiled at her. She smiled back. He knew what he must do. In a quick motion, he jumped Beckert and tried to disarm him. The Colonel was too quick, however, and shot Strong directly in the chest. Cate screamed and Mack yelled out as Strong stumbled backwards, grabbing his chest. He had never been shot in such a place. His insides felt as if they swelled up and he could feel the blood pulsating through the wound. Beckert raised his gun again and shot Strong through the head.

Strong's limp body fell back into the pool of water and he slowly sank down to the bottom. Cate cried out. It was the worst guttural scream any of the men had ever heard. Even the Nazis filling the barrels, hardened to the sounds of gunshots, stopped to look on. Mack lowered his head and put it in his hands.

Beckert smiled and holstered his Luger. He turned to his men and ordered them to continue filling the barrels.

"I didn't like doing that," Beckert told Cate and Mack. He paused for a moment, then said, "All right, I did quite enjoy it."

He pulled a small flask from his inside jacket pocket and uncorked it.

"This should be enough to see me through the next decade or so. I expect we'll see quite the war."

He walked over to the pool, knelt down and dripped the flask into the water to fill it up. As the flask bubbled and took in the aquae vitae, Beckert hummed a German tune. Cate and Mack held each other along the cave wall.

Without notice, Strong burst from the pool of water and tackled Beckert to the ground. With his hands around Beckert's neck, he squeezed as hard as he could. The Colonel gasped for air and grabbed his pistol from its holster. Strong grabbed Beckert's pistol hand and tried to gain control of it.

As Beckert and Strong fought, Ellen revealed herself from the darkness of the passageway and began firing her father's pistol. This distracted the guards and Mack tackled one of them to the ground. Retrieving his pistol, he shot the Nazi guard in the chest and then took the legs out from under the other. He followed that up with shot in the gut.

Across the cavern, the four Nazis dropped the barrels and they spilled out over the ground. Ellen turned her pistol on them and managed to take one out with a lucky shot. Mack grabbed a German rifle and fired at the Nazis.

Strong and Beckert continued fighting one another until Strong's grip overpowered Beckert's and the pistol fell to the ground. Beckert kicked Strong in the gut and rolled him off. Under the cover of his men, Beckert retreated behind a large wooden barrel. Out of bullets, Ellen ran to her father's side, where he was still firing the rifle. Beckert and his remaining three men rushed from the cavern, with two grabbing the last barrel of aquae vitae. They disappeared under heavy gunfire through the passageway from whence they had come.

Once the Nazis disappeared, Cate rushed to Strong. She grabbed him around the chest.

"I thought... I knew you were dead," Cate sobbed.

"I thought I was, too," he admitted.

Mack and Ellen rushed up to them. Ellen fell to her knees and held Father Fischer's head off the cold ground.

"It must have been the water you fell in, Harvey," said Mack. "It cured your wounds."

Strong felt his chest and Cate felt his head where he had been shot. There were no holes, no blood, nothing. It was a miracle, Strong thought.

Strong and Beckert continued fighting...

"Hurry," Ellen urged them. "Get some of that water for Father Fischer."

Mack grabbed the flask off the ground that Beckert had dropped and gave it to Ellen. She slowly poured it down the old priest's throat. After waiting a moment, nothing happened and Ellen dropped her head.

"It's too late." Ellen began to weep. Mack put his arms around her.

Suddenly, Fischer gurgled to life. He breathed in deeply, sucking in all the air his lungs could handle. Ellen rushed to give him more of the water. The priest swallowed and swallowed until he could no longer.

"Oh, thank you, Lord, Jesus Christ," said Fischer, "I am not worthy."

Ellen held the priest in her arms. Strong smiled and held Cate's body close. At that moment, he remembered Beckert and the barrel. He knew they could not return to Hitler with that jug. It would mean the end of the world as they knew it.

"We've got to go after them!"

"No, Harvey," Cate argued. "Let them go. I have all I need."

"I know, but we might not make it out unless we go now," Strong said. "They might take the torches and ladders as they go and we'd be stuck down here."

Mack chuckled, "Well, at least we have a steady supply of drinking water."

With that, the crew assembled again and prepared to make their way back out. Strong grabbed Beckert's Luger and a rifle of his own. Mack holstered his now empty pistols and grabbed a rifle. Ellen and Cate helped Father Fischer to his feet.

With a torch in hand, Strong was surprised how easy it was to navigate through the dark passageway. He remembered the Nazis did not grab a torch and would be slowed down by the darkness. As they neared the large cavern of water, Strong saw the Nazi soldiers trying to figure out how to ascend a rope ladder with a barrel of water. Strong and Mack burst through the passageway and began firing at the Nazis.

Colonel Beckert was halfway up the rope ladder barking orders. When the barrage of bullets began, he scurried up the ladder as fast as he could. He was weaponless and afraid. Strong took out two of the Nazis, both of whom fell back into the water dead. Mack tore apart the other, littering him with three or four rounds. He, too, fell dead. The barrel that they had been carrying tipped over and emptied into the pool of water. Strong dove into the water and crossed to the rope ladder. He knew Beckert would cut the ladder once he made it up.

As he ascended the ladder, Strong noticed movement in the water below him. The aquae vitae in the water had healed the wounds on two of the Nazis and they began stirring. When they surfaced, they breathed in life and caught sight of Strong halfway up the ladder. Mack tried to help his friend, but found it difficult to get a good shot. The two Nazis began to climb the ladder in an attempt to gain revenge on the man who tried to end their lives.

The closest soldier grabbed Strong's boot, but Mack managed to hit him twice in the back with the rifle. The Nazi fell back into the water. By now, the water had diluted the aquae vitae and the man had no second chance this time. The second Nazi quickly ascended the ladder now, and managed to grab both of Strong's legs. Beckert made it up and was trying to cut the rope ladder with a small pocket knife.

Strong kicked the Nazi in the head once, twice, and a third time, but the man would not give up. Mack fired twice, but did not manage to hit the soldier. He was out of ammo. The Nazi grabbed Strong's belt and started to climb on his back. Strong knew if the Nazi got to his neck, he would fall backwards and they might all become trapped inside the cavern.

Using his big elbow, Strong laid it right into the Nazi's skull once, twice, and finally a third time and the soldier let loose of Strong's belt. The man wavered for a moment and then, with a stiff kick from Strong's boot, he was propelled backward into the dark abyss. The man's head smacked against the side of the cavern and he fell limp into the water.

Strong turned his attention to the Colonel. Rung after rung, Strong made his way to the top of the ladder. Just as the rope ladder was cut loose, Strong catapulted himself up and onto the ledge above. He was met with a strong kick to the gut. Strong rolled sideways to avoid another kick and quickly jumped to his feet. He fought through the aching pain in his legs from the plane crash. That event seemed like days ago, now.

Colonel Beckert had his pocket knife in hand and easily slashed Strong's forearm. Strong stepped back and tried to conceal himself in the darkness. Beckert pulled a lighter from his pocket and struck it. It illuminated the cavern enough for him to make out Strong's silhouette in the corner. Before he knew it, however, Strong was upon him, attempting to wrestle away the pocket knife.

The lighter fell to the floor, but was still lit. Strong and Beckert's shadows danced on the wall as both men tried their damnedest to pry the blade away from the other's grip. Finally, Strong's size gave him the advantage and he kicked Beckert to the ground. Beckert scrambled to his feet and drove his body headlong into Strong's gut. Beckert's move was one of desperation and it allowed Strong to place the blade between the Colonel's lowest ribs. Strong twisted the blade and Beckert screamed out in pain. Strong felt warm blood stain his hands as he ground the blade deeper into Beckert's side.

Beckert tried to move Strong's mass, but it was too heavy with such pain in his side. Beckert tried to punch Strong in the legs, but he found those like the trunks of a great oak tree. The Colonel became a desperate animal, one who knew he was moments away from death. He would do—he had to—do anything in order to maintain his life. He grabbed Strong between the legs and twisted and hard as he could. Strong released Beckert and both men fell to the ground, panting.

"You sunovabitch…" said Strong, grabbing at his crotch. The knife had stayed in Beckert's ribs.

"*Fick dich!*" Shouted Beckert in response, spewing blood with each syllable.

Strong lifted himself up, walked to Beckert, and smacked his jaw with a right fist. Beckert responded with a left to Strong's gut. Both men then began wildly swinging, some punches connecting and others merely glancing blows. Beckert smiled, as he was schooled in boxing, and laid a right, a left, another left, and finally a right hand into the side of Strong's head. Strong wobbled backwards and caught himself on the cavern wall. Mack and the others were yelling from the cavern pool below, but neither man paid them attention. They were locked in a battle of life or death from which only one would survive.

Strong pushed off the wall and laid into Beckert with a strong right hand that glanced off his jaw and hit Beckert in the shoulder. The blow broke Strong's right hand and he fell to the ground hard. Beckert kicked Strong in the head and the big man fell onto his side.

"It seems, *mein freund*, that you have been beaten by a man out of your league," Beckert, smiled painfully. Then, he hocked bloody spittle onto Strong's back in disgust.

Beckert staggered back and reached for the knife in his side. He slowly pried it from between his ribs, groaning in agony with each twist. Finally, the knife broke free from its air pocket and Beckert was armed again. He slowly raised the knife and prepared to mercilessly end the life of the American.

"Good night, sweet prince," said Beckert.

Strong was able to look up at the dealer of death and, when it came time for his end, he clamped his eyelids shut and sucked in a large gasp of air. He waited, but nothing came. No pain, no shock, no dark end. He opened his eyes. Beckert's arms were by his side and he was just staring down at Strong. Suddenly, the knife dropped from his hand and, as he tried to muster a single word, blood gurgled from his mouth. He fell to his knees and then to his stomach, dead. A large axe was stuck into the back of his skull. The handle was carved wood and the blade was clean silver.

Strong looked up and saw the figure of a man standing above him. He had a knotted brown beard on the end of his chin. He wore skins of all sorts and was muscular. The man bent over and pulled the axe from Beckert's head. He then knelt down and looked into Strong's eyes. He seemed to be studying not only his eyes, but what lay behind them—his soul.

"*Mitt nafn er Bjarni. sál þín er hreinn. Þú getur skilið. Aldrei aftur á þennan stað,*" said the man in a deep, low tone.

Strong did not understand the man's words, but assumed Bjarni was a name of some sort, possibly his own. The bearded man sheathed his axe and disappeared into the darkness.

After a moment to find his wits and pick himself up, Strong made it to the edge of the cavern. He shouted down below and was relieved to hear Cate's voice again. After a few attempts, Mack managed to get the rope ladder up to Strong. Strong first tied the Colonel's corpse to the loose ends of the ladder for extra weight and then placed his own upper body into one of the rungs of the rope ladder and positioned himself at the edge of the precipice. This allowed Mack and the others to ascend the rope ladder and make it to the top.

When they all made it up safely, Strong began to push Beckert's body over the edge. Father Fischer yelled out and Strong stopped. Fischer searched in Beckert's jacket for a moment and then revealed the Vinland Map. He carefully placed it in his own pocket and nodded. With one good push, Beckert's body was over the edge and disappeared into the abyss. Cate then surprised him with a hug that she held for what seemed like an eternity down in the darkness. Mack grabbed Beckert's lighter from the floor of the cavern and led the group out.

When they saw the first glimpse of natural light, the whole group let out a yell of joy. Mack hooted and hollered like he was back at the *Galloping Mare*. He grabbed Ellen and hugged her tightly. Father Fischer, even at his age and being exhausted, let out a few whoops. Strong walked with his arm around Cate as they neared the gushing water of Montmorency Falls.

As Mack and Ellen made their way onto the ledge behind the falls, Father Fischer looked back into the darkness.

"What is it, Father?" Strong asked.

Fischer hesitated, then said, "It seems like we should do something to make sure nobody can get to the fountain."

"Well, you got any dynamite?" Strong suggested jokingly.

Father Fischer continued to stare, obviously worried.

"Don't worry, Father. I think there's a power here that watches over the fountain. It's in God's hands."

Strong's mention of God seemed to put Father Fischer at ease and the old priest turned and followed Ellen along the ledge. As Cate began to cross herself, Strong looked back when no one was looking.

Within that darkness, somewhere down in some musty cavern, a man waited. Strong assumed this man had been a Viking when this fountain was discovered and sacrificed his life in order to protect it, taking sips from it every so often to continue his guardianship. Looking back at Cate, he realized what a sacrifice it must be to give up any chance at friends and family. At that moment, Strong truly understood what power it was that the heart of the mountain expelled. It was the gift of God. However, it was not the gift that Strong needed or wanted. He didn't want to live forever. He just wanted to live well.

As the group passed through the Nazi encampment, they dismantled the camp and threw everything into the water. They wanted to make sure the presence of the camp did not bring fortune hunters or nosy academics to the area. They now felt it was partly their duty to protect the secret, too. At the top of Montmorency Falls, they dumped the bodies of the dead Nazis into the river and they went over the falls and were never found again. They did the same with the weapons and shell casings.

After spending the rest of the night in the cave that had saved them earlier, they buried Remy's body and made their way back to Quebec City. Once in town, they got some much needed food and rest. Mack made sure Remy's family knew he had died saving the lives of others, including a priest and young girl. He was hailed a hero in the paper.

After a few days, the group departed for home. Mack, Ellen, and Father Fischer bought their tickets for a plane bound for London. At the airport, Mack and Strong exchanged the hug of lifelong friends.

"I'm not sure the next time we'll see each other, Mack."

"Ah, I'm sure, with your luck, it won't be long, Harvey. But make sure next time you let me finish my beer."

Ellen and Cate exchanged a hug, too.

"I'm coming to visit New York next summer when my term ends," Ellen announced.

Cate smiled and Mack put an arm around his daughter.

"Does that mean you're going to enroll in college?" He questioned.

"Yeah, I am. I'm going to study ancient languages like Cate. I want more adventures."

Mack's smile left as Ellen put herself under his arm. She smiled up at him as they made their way onto the plane.

Father Fischer, who now looked a little more revived than he had in days, shook Strong's hand.

"I thank you for all of your help, Harvey. I know it was for your wife, but you did more to protect the world than you know." Fischer smiled.

"Thank you, Father. Without you, I might not have Cate right now."

Father Fischer scurried after Mack and Ellen and disappeared into the plane.

Strong and Cate stayed long enough to see their plane taxi down the runway, lift off the ground, and disappear into the clouds. Later that day, they boarded a train that took them home to New York. Cate wrote to her colleagues in Austria, telling them that she was sorry for the quick departure and that she was not going to be coming back. Strong decided it was time for him to start earning some money for the family but was not going back to the museum.

For more than a month, Strong had been locked in his study, writing. The words seemed to pour out of him like water from a mountain stream. After endless nights hunched over his desk, countless sheets of paper, and a dozen or so nibs, Strong felt it was finally complete. He dropped his pen and sat back in his chair.

Cate entered the room and walked up to him. She placed her arm around his shoulder and leaned her growing belly against him. Strong turned his head and kissed her stomach.

"Feeling sick today?" he asked.

Cate smiled, "Thankfully not. I'll be glad when this child is out and you can start sharing some of the torture." She looked down at the paper. "What did you decide for a title?"

Strong held up the top sheet. "The Adventures of Harvey Strong."

"Don't you think it's a bit vain?"

"Just a bit. But, nobody wants to read a book called, 'Fortune Seekers Who Never Find Fortune.'"

Cate laughed and pushed her belly against his head. Holding Cate and his child tightly, he was happier than he had ever been in his life. After a life out in the world, he was ready for a journey all his own. He was ready for a daily paper and family dinners instead of near-death experiences and supernatural artifacts. He knew this would be his greatest adventure all.

EPILOGUE – ONE YEAR LATER

Ellen Thatcher poured herself into the manuscript that lay on the table of the library commons. It was a few hundred years old, but the rudimentary skills she had learned in her time at college helped her discern the language. After all, she was a bright girl.

Ever since she arrived at college, she made it her goal to find the answers to her questions. Since the adventure in Quebec, her mind was a haven for mysteries and conspiracies. However, she hid her detective work from her peers, her professors, and even her father. She wasn't sure what she was dealing with yet, but didn't want anyone else to get in her way.

As Ellen flipped the page and began translating the Scottish text on the page, she slowed down. Finally! It was the breakthrough she had been waiting for. The text read:

"Summer of the First Century of the Year of Our Lord One Thousand. A trader from the islands to the South has arrived. He wears odd clothing and speaks a language unknown to all in the village. He bears a golden key and has sought refuge with Caimbeul the blacksmith."

"Finally," whispered Ellen, fingering the golden dagger key that hung about her neck.

She looked up at the large clock that hung above the commons. She was late, again. After marking the page, she closed the manuscript, placed it in her bag, and left for class.

THE END

THE SECRETS OF THE SKY TEMPLES

Greece, 1936

"Hold still!" Shouted Harvey Strong, gripping the ivory-handled straight razor as he slowly glided it down his brother's left cheek. The foamy lather disappeared with each stroke and the smooth skin beneath was revealed.

Terry Strong, twelve years younger and some pounds leaner than his elder brother, tried to stay completely still. He was gripping the seat of his chair, trying to follow his brother's advice and stay still. Around them, his bride's brothers and male cousins watched on.

"I don't see why you can't do this yourself," said Strong, wiping the blade on his pant leg and touching up a few areas on Terry's face.

"You're my *koumbaro*," said Terry, keeping his chin out. "It's tradition for the Greeks."

Strong had arrived in Piraeus, a large port city on Greece's western border, a week earlier. He had received a wedding invitation from his brother Terry, who had been working in Athens as a foreign correspondent for *The New York Tribune.* When he received the wedding notice, along with a letter from Terry asking him to be his *koumbaro* (which Strong guessed was like a best man), he knew he couldn't just forget about it. Along with Cate and their son, Terry was all the family he had left, so it was his duty to represent at the wedding. Even if it was nearly five thousand miles away.

"So when do I get to meet this bride of yours?" Strong placed the razor on the table and threw Terry a moist towel.

Terry wiped off the excess lather and inspected his clean-shaven face in the mirror. He seemed satisfied.

"I told you—she is very self-conscious of her looks. She wants the first day that you see her to be the wedding day, when she is the most beautiful."

Strong rolled his eyes. He had been in the country a week already and had not seen Terry's bride-to-be, Amara Karalis. According to Terry, they had met among mutual friends. She was a model and the daughter of a wealthy family, and very beautiful. Strong knew Terry had luck with women, but a rich model? It seemed a bit too good to be true.

"Well, isn't she a model? Doesn't she get looked at every day?" Harvey queried as the cousins and brothers inspected the groom's face and then, content, exited the room.

Terry put his jacket back on. "Yes, but she is very self-conscious, like I said.

One time, I made the mistake of asking her why her nose was a little redder than usual. She didn't speak to me for a week. She's a good woman, Harvey, just self-conscious."

After they finished, Terry walked to the balcony to smoke. Harvey followed him, pulling a flask from his vest and unscrewing the lid. Terry lit a cigarette with a fancy gold lighter and puffed. He blew the smoke out over the balcony, where the winds of the Saronic Gulf caught it and carried it out over the blue expanse. Harvey took a swig of his whiskey and screwed the lid back on his flask. He looked down at the inscription on the flask: "To Harvey. It's not going to drink itself. -Mack." He smiled. Mack had wanted to join him in Greece, but was in the midst of a divorce and had lawyers to answer to.

"Isn't it beautiful?" Terry said. Strong looked up, following Terry's eyes to the port city, its old world charm, and the blue water of the Gulf.

"Sure is, little brother."

"I never thought I'd hear that again," Terry grinned. "People here call me Strong."

"Well—in this part of the world, at least—you are. Go to Egypt, go to Portugal, there I am Strong. We are well-represented." Harvey joined Terry near the ledge.

Terry laughed. "Yeah, you've had some adventures. I was having my own here until I met Amara. Now, it seems, I'm stuck here forever."

"Having cold feet?"

"No—not really. I love her. I guess I'm just a little jealous of your situation. Getting to travel the world time and again, collecting treasures and meeting women. Drinking when you please, carrying guns…"

"Whoa, whoa, whoa. Slow it down. It's never without its dangers, Terry. All the guns, drinking, and women come at a high cost. I've lost many friends. Besides, since Henry was born, that man has turned into a father."

"I guess you're right. I'm glad you came, Harvey. I needed you here." He turned to look at Strong. Terry was the same height, but leaner. His short brown hair was curly, like their mother's had been.

"Me too. And tomorrow, we have a new member of the family."

The next day, the wedding ceremony was set up by the bride's family. Strong, as the *koumbaro*, helped get his brother dressed and placed the wedding crown on his brother's head before the ceremony. The Greeks, thought Strong, knew how to have a wedding. Crowns, spitting after each compliment, lumps of sugar—it all seemed right to him.

As the ceremony began, Strong stood next to his brother at the altar. The bride's family made up most of the wedding's guests. Strong was a little nervous, dressed up in his black suit and his brown hair combed back, standing like a present in front of all these Greeks. After the music began, supplied by a real band at the back of the church, the bride and her father entered from the far side of the church. Amara's white veil shrouded her from view until her father presented her to Terry and he flipped back her veil.

Her beauty shocked Strong. He had seen many beautiful women—Egyptian, Amazonian, Russian, and American. His wife, Cate, stunned him every day. Yet, none of them compared to Amara. She was truly a daughter of Aphrodite. Her sleek black hair was braided into a hundred tiny braids that were interwoven to create a basket weave. Her face was symmetrical, with bright pink lips and a golden smile. Her amber eyes shifted to meet Strong's and he felt her presence.

After the wedding ceremony, a grand celebration commenced. Most of the plates and bowls were destroyed and rhythmic dancing began and lasted for what seemed like hours. Finally, Terry and Amara had their dance to signify the ending of the wedding. As they danced together, people pinned money to their clothing. Strong thought this was the best part of the wedding. As the guests left, they were handed small bags of honey-dipped almonds and wished the new bride and groom luck and happiness. Strong waited for his brother to have a free moment. Finally, the last old man and woman made their way out and Strong pulled his brother to the side.

"Here," Strong handed his brother a small box.

"What's this?" Terry opened the box.

Inside, a dull gold pocket watch was lying in a bed of silk. On the watch case was intricate scrollwork and the engraving of a ship. Terry pulled it out and popped it open. Inside was an inscription: "To my husband on our wedding day. May you always keep it close. From Martha."

"It was father's," Harvey said. "Mother gave it to him on their wedding day. He used it in the Pacific."

Terry clasped the watch and then hugged his brother. Strong grabbed his brother close and squeezed him, too. It had been some years since they embraced. Strong felt like it might be years until they did again, but he hoped it wasn't true. After a moment, they let each other go and Terry left with his bride. Strong shed his fancy suit like a snake sheds his skin and went for a walk near the water. After a while, he stumbled upon a small bar and stopped for a drink. He stayed there until the night waned and then went back to his room for some sleep. He was leaving for America tomorrow.

When Strong awoke, it was not by the sun creeping up to his face through the blinds or the smell of hot tea or coffee waking his nose, but by his brother, Terry, shaking him into the waking world.

"What—what's going on?" asked Strong, with a bit of frustration in his words. He remembered he had a twelve hour flight ahead of him.

"Harvey, get up, please," Terry pleaded anxiously. "I need help."

Strong lifted from his back and sat on the edge of his bed. "What?"

"Someone broke in last night—into our room."

"What—are you okay? Is Amara okay?"

"No—I mean, yes, she's okay. I'm okay. But they left this note on our bed." He showed Harvey the note. It read that if the sender didn't receive their payment, they would take payment in the form of his new bride. Strong turned to Terry and frowned. Terry stared at his brother, looking confused.

"Don't give me that look, Terry, I know this is your doing."

"What? Me? You think I wanted someone to break in on my wedding night?"

"No. But I know you must have had something to do with the reason they did. Tell me."

Terry hesitated for a moment, standing up and pacing around the room. He held the note tight in his hands. He sighed and rubbed his eyes. Strong noticed Terry was wearing part of his suit from last night.

"Look, I may have gotten into a little bit of debt," Terry finally admitted.

Strong jumped up and grabbed his brother, saying, "I knew it! Damnit, Terry, I knew it. With who—for what?"

"Gambling."

Strong gnashed his teeth together. "Gambling? Again?"

"Yes, I'm sorry. There's nothing to do around here. So, naturally, I picked up a pastime," Terry confessed.

"Yeah—a pastime? Do you remember why you can't enter Italy again without Papal approval?" Strong shouted. He lowered his voice to avoid startling anyone nearby.

"I'm sorry, Harvey, I am. I thought they wouldn't track me from Athens, but I guess they did."

"Hell, the wedding notices might have alerted them," Strong guessed.

Terry lowered his head, realizing his stupidity. Strong released his brother and sat back on the bed. He rubbed his eyes and sighed. Terry looked nervous.

"Well—what do you owe?"

"About twenty thousand drachmas. That's maybe, six or seven hundred dollars."

"Are you kidding me? Seven hundred dollars? Oh my god, Terry. Who do you owe this to?"

"I'm not sure exactly who they are, but they call themselves the Cult of the Builder. They are low-key gangsters who run booze and loan money."

"Great—only gangsters and loan sharks." Strong pulled out his suitcase and threw it on the bed. He began pulling his clothes from the closet and throwing them inside. Terry watched in disbelief.

"What are you doing, Harvey?"

"Leaving, before you suck me into your pile of shit."

"You can't leave!" Terry grabbed Strong's arm. Strong turned and punched him in the face. Terry fell to the floor and blood trickled from his busted lip. "She's my wife, Harvey. They said they would take her if we don't pay them back."

"Just leave the country, like everyone else with debts."

"I can't. Don't you see? My wife's family is here and she would never leave."

"Then leave her here." The moment he said it, Strong knew Terry could not. Hell, if Strong was in his shoes, he wouldn't leave Amara, either. She was too rare a shell to leave on the beach. Terry would protect her until his death. It was her skill, her power, over men.

"I don't have the money." Strong sat back on the bed.

Terry slowly lifted himself up off the floor. "I know. If you would just help me talk to these guys, maybe broker another arrangement for us. That's all I ask, Harvey, then you can leave. Think of it as a wedding present."

Strong contemplated saying, "No." Yet, he knew that whatever happened to Terry was his responsibility, in this situation, at least. Strong knew Terry. He didn't have a bad bone in his body, but was easily swindled. As his older brother, and the more experienced of the two, Strong had to see this through. The quicker is was over and done with, the sooner he could get home to Cate and their son.

"All right, let's get this done," he conceded. Terry smiled and hugged him. For some reason, Strong thought, it didn't feel like the hug the night before.

The next day, Harvey and Terry borrowed a car from Amara's father. According to Terry, her father was a wealthy ship builder. Their family had built ships during the Greek War of Independence. Now, they owned nearly every major shipyard in the port city of Piraeus. The car was a bright red Lincoln Sport, nicer than anything Strong had ever driven. Terry was giving him directions through the city. They were heading to the southern part of Athens, where Terry had last seen the members of the Cult of the Builder.

"Why do they call themselves that—Cult of the Builder?" Strong's long hair was ruffled in the wind of the speeding convertible.

"I'm not sure," Terry replied. "When the Greeks say 'cult' it's like saying group or organization. Who the Builder is, I don't know."

They drove for nearly an hour, passing villages that paled in comparison to the vistas of Piraeus. Poor merchants lined the sides of the road halfway out of town to try and sell their handmade wares. Strong wondered what their lives were like, setting up a stand day after day, selling the same things for the same money. It wasn't the life he'd would ever want, but it was interesting to think about. Soon, they arrived at Petralona, a neighborhood of Athens. Terry told Strong to turn left down a street lined with tall buildings.

There were hardly any alleyways between them, as they were seemingly crammed together with each new addition. After a moment, they pulled the car over to the side of the street and got out. Strong followed Terry down the block until they came to a gap in the buildings. Neither of the adjacent buildings had signs or markers telling patrons what or if they were businesses. Strong suspected they were not owned by well-to-do businessmen. As they walked down the alleyway, Terry stopped at a door to their left. It was a large wooden door with a metal plate covering the peep hole. There was no door handle. Terry kicked the door twice with his foot.

After a moment, the metal latch slid open and the eyes of a man appeared at the peep hole. He had a large scar across his face: starting over his left eyebrow, going over his nose, and down to his right jaw line. He huffed and said, "Poios eísai?"

Terry had been in Greece for nearly three years. He replied, in hesitant Greek, "*Eímai* Terry Strong. *Eímai edó gia na plirósei to chréos mou pros ton k Anágnos.*"

The man huffed again and turned his gaze to Strong. "*Poiós eínai aftos?*"

Terry replied, "*O aderfós mou.*"

Satisfied, the man closed the latch and opened the door. Once in full view, the door watcher was a spectacle to behold. He wore gray suit pants and a white shirt with no sleeves. Either they had cut off or had ripped off from his immense arm muscles. He was not very tall, but was well-built and looked like an Olympic wrestler. The man motioned them in and they followed. They walked down a long hallway, dimly lit by the sparse lights that lined the hallway wall. They passed numerous doors, some open and some shut. Once, he saw a half-naked woman lying on a bed, smoking a long cigarette. In another room, three old men were praying to a shrine. To Strong, this was a circus. Finally, they came to the last door at the end of the hall and the big man checked Strong and Terry for weapons. He didn't find anything. Strong felt his .38 snub nose pistol rub against his ankle as he walked into the room.

Inside the room was a large, square desk and behind it sat a man who Strong guessed was the leader of this group. He wore a fine gray silk suit and a gray fedora on his head. He smoked on a cigar and had a bottle of wine on his desk.

Two men stood at either side of the desk, both carrying pistols at their hips. Strong looked around the room. Large paintings adorned the walls, some of which Strong recognized. He noticed an oil painting of Oedipus, Dionysus offering a young man fruit, and finally, behind the man's desk, the largest painting of all: a dark, ominous painting of a large man wielding a hammer, forging something on an anvil.

Terry was shoved from behind by the guard and he fell to his knees. Then the thug grabbed Terry around the neck and began choking him. Strong was tempted to stop him, but knew it was the cost of playing with other people's money.

"Where is my money, Mr. Strong?" Asked the man behind the desk. His words were deep and followed by large puffs of smoke as they exited his throat.

"Mr. Anagnos, I'm sorry I'm so late, I meant to write," Terry gasped as the guard squeezed tighter.

Strong put his hands in his pockets and watched silenty.

"You ran from me, you little *malaka!*" Snappped Anagnos, rising from his chair and slamming his fists on his desks. The men beside him budged for a second, but found their footing.

"I'm sorry. I will do anything you..." Terry began, but Strong cut him off.

"No, he won't," Strong corrected keeping his eyes on Anagnos.

Anagnos slowly turned his head and glared at Strong. "What did you say to me?"

"I know my little brother," Strong continued. "And he won't do anything you ask."

Anagnos looked like he might pull a gun and shoot everyone in the room. His face turned bright red and he did not breathe. He walked out from behind the desk and slowly shuffled his way to Strong. He was not a large man, but looked like he could give, and take, a punch. In fact, the scars on his face and his wilted nose looked like he might have done that more than once in his life. He stared up at Strong. Their eyes met.

"You're right," he concurred. "I'm Adelphos Anagnos, leader of the Clan of the Builder. I have a brother, too, and do not hold yours against you."

Strong shook Anagnos' hand and smiled. "If he were, I would be a dead man already."

"I see which one of you got the brains... and the braun," Anagnos chuckled, looking Strong up and down.

At that moment, a man burst through the door. All three bodyguards pulled their pistols and pointed them at the intruder. The man fell to the floor. He was wearing tattered clothing and had at least three wounds on his torso. His face was badly beaten. He moaned in pain. Anagnos knelt down and lifted the man's head.

"*Ti tréchei? Poios to ékane aftó?*" Asked Anagnos.

The man slowly replied, "*Emeís éprepe , afentikó. To píran.*"

"Who?" Anagnos inquired in English.

"The Warden," the man answered. With that, he sighed and breathed his final breath.

Anagnos laid his head down and then motioned for the two bodyguards to take care of his body. Anagnos returned to his desk and picked up his bent cigar. He puffed on it a few times, staring up at the painting behind his desk. He turned and looked at Strong and Terry.

"You owe me money," he said.

"I know, but I…" began Terry, but Anagnos raised his hand stopped him.

"It was wrong of me to threaten the life of your new bride. For that, I apologize. However, you do owe me money and I want to see it paid back."

"We don't have the money, Mr. Anagnos," Harvey injected.

"I know you don't," Anagnos nodded. "But I know you have skills and experience, Mr. Strong."

Strong was shocked. "Me?"

"Yes. Harvey Strong: adventurer extraordinaire. Men told me of your escapades in Thebes and Antilla."

"How did you…?"

"I have men everywhere in the world. Even in New York," Anagnos declared. "In lieu of my owed money, I ask for your services for a time."

"Doing what?" Strong's eyebrows arched.

"There is something that belongs to me that has been stolen. I want you to retrieve it for me."

"What is it?" squealed Terry, still being choked by the door watcher. The door watcher clenched his elbow and Terry squirmed.

Anagnos turned to look at the painting behind his desk. "We are the Cult of the Builder. We are a group devoted to honoring the legend of Hephaestus, the Greek god of blacksmiths, craftsmen, sculptors, and fire. He crafted the weapons of the gods on Mount Olympus. While many of the stories are legend, some are found in truth."

Anagnos pulled a box from his desk and walked over to Strong. "Hephaestus was married to Aphrodite, goddess of love and beauty, but she was unfaithful. She lay with Ares, god of war, and Hephaestus found them in bed together. While he was offered payment by Ares, Hephaestus could not forgive Aphrodite, as she bore Ares' child: Harmonia. For her wedding day, Hephaestus crafted a fine necklace of solid gold. The greatest craftsman in the world, Hephaestus could make anything from his hammer and anvil. Into this necklace, he laid

"The Warden," the man answered.

a curse: the wearer would be eternally beautiful and young, but would bring ruin to her husband and house."

Anagnos opened the box and inside it was empty. He showed it to Strong.

"For thousands of years, this necklace passed from house to house, bringing ruin to each and every one of them. In the late 1500's, a group of like-minded individuals banded together to take the necklace and keep it secure. This was the Cult of the Builder. The Builder is Haephestus. We honor his power and craftsmanship, but not the evil that he poured into the necklace. Until recently, we had guarded the necklace safely for nearly four hundred years."

Strong spoke up, "Who has it?"

Anagnos closed the box and walked back to his desk.

"That—I do not know. I sent my men to try to retrieve it, but they were unsuccessful, as you just witnessed. We know the necklace is somewhere in Glyfada, to the south. That is all."

"If I can get you this necklace, will my brother's debts be forgiven?"

"If you can get me the necklace, then I will personally see to the safety of him, his children, and his house for as long as the Cult exists."

Outside on the street, Strong and Terry walked to the car.

"Thank you, Harvey, I…"

"I'm not sure we will be able to find the necklace, so you might want to hold off on the thanks, little brother."

They reached the Lincoln and jumped in. They were planning to head back to the villa to change clothes and get some gear before leaving for Glyfada. As they sped off toward Piraeus, a figure popped up in the backseat.

"Hey!"

The unexpected passenger startled Terry, who was driving, and he swerved, taking out a sign on the side of the street and almost running over a group of tourists. Strong reached down and pulled his .38 pistol from his leg. He turned and pointed at the passenger, expecting an assassin or one of Anagnos' men. It was Amara. Her black hair was in a ponytail and she was wearing a white blouse. It contrasted her dark, sun-kissed skin. When Terry realized who it was by using the rear-view mirror, his jaw dropped.

"Amara—What are you doing here?"

"I am coming with you," she said.

"No—you are not," Strong countered as he holstered his pistol.

"Yes I am. Don't think you are going to run off with my husband to America and leave me here with my father." Her brown eyes lit up like fired jewels. Strong stared into them.

"What?" Terry blurted.

"What are you talking about?" Strong queried.

Amara looked at both men. Her face got red. "Aren't you running off?" Terry smiled, "No, my dear. We aren't running off. We had some business to handle."

"Oh—well. I don't know what to say, then." She sat back against the leather seats and went silent.

Terry smiled. "I'm glad to know that…"

Instantly, the back end of the Lincoln was jolted by a large truck behind them. The car skidded sideways. Everyone was jostled inside and Terry tried to hold on to the steering wheel. After a second, he managed to straighten the car and he punched the gas.

"Who the hell is it?" Terry shouted.

"I don't know, but let's not stick around to find out," Harvey advised.

Strong pulled his pistol again and twisted around. He told Amara to duck down. He pointed the pistol at the truck behind them and fired a shot. It missed the front windshield, but nicked the side mirror. The truck swerved and then rammed the Lincoln again. Amara was trying her best to grab onto something in the back seat while Terry was trying to watch the road and the rear view mirror at the same time. Strong ripped the rear-view mirror off.

"Watch the front. I've got the back," he orderd.

Strong turned around and fired another shot. It hit the windshield, but the bullet did not break the glass. Strong fired two more shots and the windshield busted into four pieces. A man in the passenger seat kicked it out. The truck sped up again and rammed the Lincoln a third time. The truck stayed close enough for the passenger to crawl out where the windshield had been and jump onto the back of the Lincoln. The man kicked the gun from Strong's hand and it flew out of the car. Strong jumped up onto the seat and dove at the man. The two of them skidded across the trunk and almost right off the car. Strong's feet managed to grab the edge of the back seat and keep from falling to the road.

Terry swerved again and Strong and his attacker slid to the other side of the trunk. Strong punched the man in the face. On his second attempt, the man dodged the blow and Strong punched the hard metal body of the car. As he writhed in pain, the man dealt a blow to Strong's jaw and he fell into the back seat. Amara screamed as the man grabbed her by the hair. Terry turned away from the wheel and dove at the fellow. He tackled the man as the car swerved uncontrollably from side to side. Strong grabbed the wheel just in time to swerve away from a small cafe.

Terry and their foe fought standing in the back seat of the Lincoln. The man grabbed Terry around the neck and tried to push him from the moving car, but Amara jumped on the man's back and began strangling him. Terry punched the man in the face and he fell back into the seat, squishing Amara.

"We're running out of road," shouted Strong, pointing to a dead end and the side of the brick building ahead of them.

Terry pulled the thug off Amara, punched him once more, and threw him from the car. The brute hit the pavement and flipped a few times before going limp on the sidewalk. The truck behind them sped up attempting to ram them again. Somehow, Strong managed to wheel the car out of the way before it could hit them. Terry jumped in the front seat next to his brother's tenacity.

"Let me drive," he yelled. Strong was impressed by his little brother.

Terry and Strong switched and, just before they hit the wall, Terry skidded the car sideways and they squeezed through an opening between two buildings. The truck behind them attempted the same maneuver, but was top heavy and flipped onto its side. Terry and Strong shouted in excitement as they drove away. Amara lifted up from the backseat and sighed, her hair a mess. The three of them drove off south toward the villa.

Back at Terry's in-laws, the three of them snuck the beat up Lincoln into the covered drive on the side of the main house.

"Don't worry," said Amara, "I'll tell my father I took it for a joyride."

Strong smiled and then noticed Terry looking at him. Strong's face returned to normal. Amara led them rear entrance and, once inside, they all sat down on plush chairs. Strong sighed, thinking about his lost pistol. Terry grabbed Amara and kissed her.

"You were amazing out there, Amara." She smiled and placed a hand on his chest as he held her close.

"What was all that about anyway?" she asked.

"Nothing," Strong shrugged. "Just some thugs."

"I know Greek thugs, Harvey," Amara retorted. "And those were not Greek thugs."

"She deserves to know, Harvey," Terry argued. "After all, she's my wife, now."

Strong reluctantly conceded and they filled Amara in on the meeting with Anagnos and the quest they had undertaken to find the necklace of Harmonia. Strong noticed that Terry left out the part about his gambling debts. Terry conviced Amara they were doing this for fortune and glory. Strong did not expose the lie, as he figured it would do more harm than good.

"So, Glyfada," Terry continued. "Do you know that area, darling?"

Amara was fixing the men's drinks. "Yes. Not well, but my uncle oversees one of my father's shipyards there. He can help us."

Strong spoke up, "We're going to need guns."

Amara smiled. "I think I need to show you my father's favorite room."

After handing them their glasses of whisky, Amara led them upstairs to a special room. She opened the door and Strong's eyes lit up. Inside was every gun he had ever heard of, aside from the larger machine guns and turrets. Strong inspected the glass cabinets, noticing all makes and models of rifles, handguns, and even melee weapons. He stopped when he saw a Winchester Model 1873. He looked the gun up and down.

"Ah, that's an original," Amara pointed out. My father bought it at auction a few years ago. It's never been fired."

"That's about to change," Strong grinned.

Amara allowed the men to pick two weapons each, enough for their trip but not enough that her father would notice upon a quick glance. Strong chose the Winchester '73 and a Webley Mark 6. Terry chose a double-barreled shotgun and Colt 1911.

Strong eyed Terry's shotgun. "Plan on driving a stagecoach anytime soon, brother?"

Terry smirked, "With you around, you never know."

The three of them loaded up their gear and took a more inconspicuous black Ford. Strong and Terry piled in the front seat, with Amara in the back. On the road to Glyfada, Strong and Terry strategized for their arrival in the southeastern suburb of Athens. Terry had an old gambling friend living in Glyfada that he figured could point them in the direction of the local "market." Strong figured his brother had an affinity to finding trouble, so he would let Terry do the navigating. Sooner or later, they would run into it.

An hour later, the trio arrived at the outskirts of Glyfada. The seaside town was not at luxurious as Pireaus, but the buildings were much more packed together and the amount of people squirming about on the streets seemed to double. The sun was slowly setting overhead, and as they drove deeper into the city, the people seemed to become more and more suspicious of the car. Terry took a left turn down a side street and stopped out in front of what looked to Strong like a brothel.

"Didn't you say this guy was a racehorse breeder?" Harvey asked.

"Ah....yes, in his spare time. Mostly Lawrence runs brothels and gambling houses. That's where he makes his real money."

Strong stepped out the car and followed Terry. He left the long gun in the car, but the Mark VI hung in his hip inside his belt. Amara quickly stepped after them.

"Lawrence? That doesn't sound like a Greek name," Strong noted.

"No, he's not. Originally from England. Might remind you of your old pal Mack a bit."

"No one's like Mack."

The trio entered the front door and Strong noticed the pungent smell of perfume lining the air inside. It hit his nostrils like a baseball bat and he coughed slightly. The walls were lined with all styles of draperies and lavish couches and chairs lined the floor. A Madame approached them wearing a see-through cloak that left nothing to the imagination. A few half-nude women walked past the trio. Amara was obviously trying not to look around, as was Terry.

"What can I do for you, gentlemen?" The Madame, puffing on a long, white cigarette. She blew smoke into the air above their heads.

"We're here to see Lawrence. I'm Terry Strong."

"And your friend? Does he need company while you speak to Mr. Gosling?" wondered the Madame, pointing her cigarette at Strong.

"No," said Strong, "I will be joining him."

"You haven't yet seen our selection." The Madame pointing to a room behind her to the right.

"I'm good," Strong smiled. "Besides, I'm broke."

"Then, by all means," she pointed to a staircase behind her, "Mr. Gosling's office is upstairs. Please use the side entrance if you are not here for business."

The Strong brothers walked past her but Harvey noticed Amara was not following. Terry turned and saw the Madame had grabbed Amara's arm and was looking her up and down.

"My dear. You are an exquisite beauty. Too beautiful to be kept upstairs. Can I interest you in a job? You will be a rich woman inside a year."

Amara blushed. "No, thank you. I'm already rich."

Terry walked back and took hold of Amara's elbow. "And already married."

"A shame," the woman sighed. "Such a model of Aphrodite should not be wasted on one man."

The trio continued up the stairs, finally reaching a door at the top. Terry knocked once and then entered. Strong and Amara followed him.

Inside, a group of half-nude women covered in lavish robes, most see-through material, were sitting around drinking. At the other end of the carpeted room, a large, burly man was sitting on a couch being fed by a completely nude woman. When the door opened, he peered across the room and smiled. The nude woman tried to feed him another grape, but he pushed her hand away and sat up.

A loose towel fell from his waist and his nakedness shocked Amara. She quickly turned her head away, as did Strong. Terry stepped forward with open arms.

"Lawrence, how the hell are you, old friend!"

A man of about forty, Lawrence had grape juice stains down his chin and chest, staining his blonde beard bright purple.

"Terry fucking Strong, how the hell are you, my friend?" The two old friends hugged.

After Terry gave Lawrence a short introduction to his older brother and new wife, he enlightened Lawrence on why they were there.

"So, you are looking for this necklace, hmm?" Pondered Lawrence, rubbing his beard, "I have not heard of the necklace, but there is someone who may know. I warn you though: she's a feisty one."

"What do you mean? Who is she?" Terry gave Harvey a puzzled look.

"Not sure, Terry. She came here a few weeks back peddling some key she had found and I turned her away. I have no interest in keys. Me? I like coin and books. That is where the long value is, my friend," Lawrence reported.

"So what makes you think she'd be of help to us?" Strong, butted into the conversation. He found it hard not to be the main investigator.

Lawrence turned to him directly. "Like I said, she had this key. She was inquiring about something I have no need for. Now, you show up asking me about something I have no need for. I just put two and two together."

Strong sat back in his chair. He did not see the use for Lawrence or his information. He stood and began walking toward the door. Terry called out, but Strong kept walking. He was tired of waiting around, of the gunfights, of the loose ends. He wanted to go home.

Strong walked down the stairs and bypassed the Madame at the bottom. He burst through the front doors and into the street. He stared up into the sky and sighed. This was too much. When he saw Terry, he would wish him luck and be on his way home. This was the life for a young man, not a father.

After a moment, Terry and Amara appeared through the doors behind him. Strong scratched his chin, trying to think of the best words to say.

"What the hell, Harvey?" Terry shoved his older brother in the shoulder. "Why did you storm off like that?"

"I can't do this, Terry. I'm a father now. I need to go home."

"Then go, Harvey!"

Amara stepped between the brothers. "Stop it! Both of you! This bickering is unbearable."

Harvey and Terry were silenced by Amara's words. They stared down at their shoes.

"You are brothers. Terry: you know Harvey has a life aside from this. Be patient with him. He is helping us out of this mess. Harvey: please reconsider. We need your help here."

After a moment, Harvey spoke up. "Fine. Terry, tell me where we're going?"

"Lawrence gave me a name and an address: West side of Glyfada, her name is Ellen Thatcher."

Strong found himself wondering how in the world Ellen Thatcher had made it to Glyfada, Greece, and, more importantly, why she was involved in antiquities dealings. The last he heard, she was at college in London.

As the trio followed Lawrence's directions to the west side of Glyfada, Strong relayed to Terry and Amara the adventure he had with Ellen a couple of years back. Amara found such a young girl interesting, but Terry couldn't imagine it.

A twenty minute drive later, the trio found themselves in the right place. The long, narrow street ahead of them was crowded with tables and vendors. The general buzz of conversation made the place sound like a warzone. Terry pulled the car over and they exited the vehicle.

"All right, so we're looking for a vendor named Mistress Shek. She's the one who Ellen has been staying with here," said Terry.

Strong led the way down the narrow aisles, looking side-to-side for a Mistress Shek. As he looked, he noticed numerous artifacts of gold, silver, and precious gems. He wondered how many were real. In his experience with such places, you had a better chance of finding clean water than a real artifact.

As Amara walked closely behind Terry, the vendors took a keen eye to her. They tried to sway her to buy a beautiful headpiece, or a gold-plated bracelet, or a brush set from the Greek Islands. She smiled and continued walking, never replying to their heckling.

As they rounded a bend in the market, Terry pointed to a building behind the market to the right.

"Look! Up there."

Strong followed his brother's pointing and saw an old, dusty sign that read: "Ms. Shek, Boarding House."

"I take it that's what we're looking for," Harvey stated.

The trio weaved their way through the market and up the old brick steps to

"...we're looking for a vendor named Mistress Shek."

Mistress Shek's boarding house. Inside, they were met by a bellhop at the front desk who welcomed them to Ms. Shek's. They inquired about Ellen Thatcher, but the bellhop was not aware of such a name. A stranger in the corner of the room lifted his head at the name. He was reading a paper and smoking a cigarette. When Strong and crew were unsure of what to do next, the stranger dropped the paper and walked up to them.

In the light, the stranger's face was illuminated. He was not Greek. He had a reddish goatee and a long, lean face. His eyes were blue. "Lady, gentlemen, I see you need assistance finding someone." By his distinct accent, he was clearly Scottish.

Strong turned to the man and was immediately wary of his intentions. Anyone who volunteered their assistance was to be vetted first.

"Who are you?" Strong asked.

Amara cut him off. "Yes, we do. We are looking for Ellen Thatcher. She's English and is reportedly trying to find information about a key."

Strong turned to Amara and gave her a stern look. He did not like giving away their information so openly to strangers.

The stranger smiled. "Ah, I see. Well, I may be able to help."

Terry butted in, "All right, how much?"

"Who are you?" Strong added.

"I'm sorry gentlemen, one at a time, please. To answer your question, sir, I am Lachlan Campbell. And to you, sir, I do not charge for my services. I am an expatriot living here in Glyfada and I have nothing better to do."

"Cut the shit," Strong wasn't convinced. "You either want money or something else in this world. I've been everywhere, seen everything, and never met someone willing to give anything for free."

Campbell thought for a moment, puffing his cigarette. He turned to Amara and confessed. "All right, you have me in a corner. I admit that I did not intend to simply give you my assistance. This Ellen Thatcher, she stole something from me. A key. It is dagger-shaped and has large teeth on the end."

Strong didn't believe Ellen was a thief. Yet, again, he didn't know the girl all too well anymore. The man's story made sense, but probably wasn't the entire truth. It's possible he wanted the key for himself.

Amara was more receptive. "Then I think we can work something out."

After that, Terry relayed what they were looking for and why to Lachlan Campbell. The Scot puffed on his cigarette with each new piece of information. He seemed like a trustworthy fellow to Terry and Amara, but Strong still wasn't sold. When the story finished, Campbell spoke up.

"Well, I can tell you, whatever Anagnos has told you is a lie."

Harvey puzzled. "What do you mean?"

"Anagnos is known as a liar and a cheat in Greece. Don't you wonder why he sent you on some wild goose chase for this necklace when he could just seize your assets to make up his cash? He sucks people in, makes them in his debt, and then sends them to do his dirty work."

"I don't know," Terry mused. "Anagnos has always been fair to me. I owe him money, plain and simple."

"Terry, we should listen to this man, he has not wronged us yet," Amara argued. Her eyes were full of life.

Her new husband shrugged. "All right, go on, Campbell. Tell us more."

"Those men you speak of, the ones who attacked your earlier? Your description is exactly like those of Anagnos."

"So you're saying Anagnos sent those men to kill us?" Strong was getting annoyed. "Why would he do that?"

"That, I do not know, but Anagnos is tricky. One moment he wants something, the other he wants you dead."

"What next?" Terry queried. "Where do we go to find Thatcher?"

"Just yesterday I heard tell of a young white woman travelling out of town heading to the north. They said she chartered a plane to Meteora."

"Meteora?" Harvey uttered. "What's that?"

"Meteora is the monastery in the sky," Amara explained. "Stone pillars and hills that jut out of the landscape that some say were raised by the gods. There are monasteries built on top."

"Exactly," Campbell nodded. "And some say they have ancient relics hidden there. I think this Thatcher believes her key plays some role in that place. I also wonder if your necklace could be hidden within the walls of Meteora."

With that, Strong, Terry, Amara, and their new guide, Campbell, chartered their own plane to Meteora. Before leaving, Strong stopped at the communications office to send word to Cate that he would be longer away than he had anticipated. Hopefully, she would understand.

A few hours later, their small plane landed in the Greek town of Trikala, the closest they could get to the sky temples without landing right on top of a mountain. Strong and Terry managed to conceal their weaponry in their luggage, and made sure Campbell did not know they were armed. When they arrived, Strong tucked the Webley Mark VI in his waistband.

As they climbed the long trek up to the temples at Meteora, Strong felt a suspicion that they were being followed. While he didn't believe entirely the story about Anagnos and his deception, Strong didn't put it past the Greek gangster to double cross them. Especially an outsider who owed him money.

After a half hour, Amara needed a rest, so the group stopped on the outskirts of the town called Kalabaka. It was the nearest civilization to the temples and the last they would see of people until they returned. While Amara used the bath house afforded to her by her father's money, Strong and Terry chatted outside away from Campbell.

"I don't know about this Scot, Terry," Strong began leaning in and whispering to his brother.

"What do you mean, Harvey? He hasn't led us astray yet?"

"Would a butcher lead a group of hogs astray? No, they follow blindly to their deaths," He made a cutting motion across his neck.

"I know you have more experience in this type of situation, Harvey, but I really think Campbell wants us to find Thatcher."

"I agree, but I don't think it's because of us. I think there is something he's not telling us. When there's an opportunity, he's going to try and separate us up at the temples. Be careful if we are."

"You're overreacting, big brother, but I will."

Campbell came around the corner of the building and they stopped talking. The Scot eyed them and smirked.

"You planning to leave me behind, gents?" he asked, rubbing his red goatee.

"No," said Terry, "why would we do that?"

"So, Campbell," Strong redirected the conversation. "Tell me more about why you're after this Thatcher woman. Is it the key?"

"Yes, the key, exactly. This key belonged to my father and my father's father in Scotland. It belonged to the head of my clan for generations. Nearly a thousand years ago, it was stolen from us by invaders. Now Thatcher has it, and I'd like to get it back."

"Interesting story. So you think, just because she has it, that she knowingly stole it? What if she bought it on the market?"

"I see your point. Yes, to a certain degree, I understand. I don't want to hurt or jail this woman. I just want the key back."

"What was it for, this key?" Strong pressed.

"You wouldn't believe me, if I told you."

"Shoot."

At that moment, Amara appeared from the bathhouse. Terry jumped up and walked over to her. Strong watched as Campbell followed the interaction of Terry and his wife. Strong wondered who this man truly was.

Strong grabbed his pack and threw it on his back. Suddenly, a gun rang out in the outskirts of town and a bullet lodged itself in the clay building next to him. He dropped to the ground, as did Campbell. Terry pushed Amara behind the building and dove after her. More bullets whizzed through the buildings and people began running and screaming in panic.

Strong wasn't yet ready to reveal that he was armed. He yelled out, "What do we do here, Campbell?"

From his stomach, Campbell looked around and then caught sight of the high stone pillars rising up from the earth behind the town. He looked back at Strong. "Our only chance it to make a run for it through town to the temples. It will be more difficult traversing the open land, but we won't be dead."

Terry yelled out, "I agree! Let's go."

The others waited for Strong's opinion. After some thinking, he decided it was their best option. He shook his head and then, in a quick motion, everyone jumped up and sprinted toward the temples.

Bullets whizzed by them as the group ran as fast as they could, dodging screaming townspeople, sheep, and carts piled up between buildings.

Terry tripped over something in the midst of the action and fell to the dirt. Strong stopped, and so did Amara. Strong yelled for her to keep going.

"Get up!" Harvey yelled grabbing his brother by the arm.

From the side of a building, a man appeared holding a rifle. Strong dove for him and shoved backward into the building. The rifle dropped out of the man's hands and Strong head butted him. The man fell to the ground like a sack of Greek coins. Strong turned just in time for Terry to get to his feet. They burst into a run again after Campbell and Amara. As they rounded another building, Strong noticed Amara and Campbell were stopped in the middle of a small courtyard. Strong grabbed his brother's shirt and yanked him behind a building.

"What are you doing?" Terry shouted.

Strong shushed him and whispered, "They are trapped. Being trapped with them won't help get them out."

Terry and Strong peered out from behind the building. In the courtyard, a group of men held Amara and Campbell at gunpoint. One of the men walked up to Campbell and smacked him across the face. The man wore two pistols on his waist belt and a gray suit much like Anagnos. For a moment, Strong believed Campbell's suspicions about Anagnos' were valid.

"That's my wife, Harvey, I've got to help her," Terry pleaded.

"I know, I know. I've been there, kid. But you need to wait until the right time."

Strong turned Terry's attention back to the courtyard. It looked like the men were leading Amara and Campbell to several trucks on the roadway. It reminded Strong of the one that had attacked them in the city days earlier. Soon enough, the captives were loaded in the back the largest truck, along with the man in the gray suit and eight armed guards. The other men loaded into a smaller truck and took off south, away from the temples. The truck with Amara and Campbell fired up and slowly started up the incline of the mountain toward the temples.

"We can't let those trucks get away or we'll be hours behind them." Strong motioned to Terry to follow him.

They ducked behind a peddler's cart for a moment until the smaller truck heading south went by them. Right after, they took off toward the truck with the captives on board. Strong ran as fast as his bulk would go, with Terry staying close behind.

"Try to jump and hold on to the rear bumper of the truck! Make sure they don't see you in the side mirrors!" Strong shouted.

Terry nodded as they neared the edge of the truck. Strong pinpointed where both of his hands would latch onto and then dove with all the momentum that he could muster. His hands, strong and well-versed in such skill, latched onto the bumper and his lower body dragged behind in the dirt. Terry dove after Strong, but his momentum did not carry him to the bumper. Instead, he grabbed onto Strong's lower body.

"Terry! What the hell!" Strong tried his best to hold on while Terry tried to climb up to the bumper.

Luckily for them both, Strong was a large man and his body could handle the added weight of his younger brother. Slowly, but surely, Terry managed to climb up to the bumper and then grabbed it for himself. Then, they both used their upper body strength to lift themselves onto the bumper and were able to cling on with their bodies like monkeys to a swaying tree. Terry smiled at Strong, who did not return the favor.

Ten minutes later, the truck was at the pinnacle of the mountain. It stopped and the Strong brothers dropped from the bumper and rolled underneath the truck. The guards pulled Amara and Campbell from the back of the truck and pushed them toward the bridge that connected the road to the monasteries situated across a deep gorge. After a moment, the driver and the man in the gray suit stepped out, as well. They followed the group toward the bridge.

Strong shuffled his body across the dirt underneath the truck and looked out. He was amazed at what he saw. The huge stone pillars were like floating clouds of earth that God himself had raised up from the ground. He imagined peering over the edge and seeing into Hell's mouth. Strong wasn't afraid of heights, after all he had been through, but the temples in the sky were a sight to behold. He wondered what it might have been to visit them as a tourist.

"*Thátser échei diameínei sto kentrikótero naó,*" said the man in the gray suit as he walked away from the truck.

Strong whispered to Terry, "What did he say?"

Terry tried to translate in his head. "Something about Thatcher and the center temple. Beyond that, I'm not exactly sure. My Greek is mediocre, at best."

Terry pointed to the guards on the bridge. They crossed slowly, making sure that Amara and Campbell did not have a chance to escape. At the other side of the bridge, the men knocked on the door of the first temple. A small monk opened the door and made some sort of greeting to the group. The man in the gray suit hit the monk across the head and he fell to the ground. At that moment, Strong's anger for Anagnos and his men swelled up and he vowed to make them pay. Soon, they were inside and out of sight.

Strong rolled out from under the truck and Terry followed him.

"If they mentioned the center temple, that must be where they're going. We need to get there first in case Ellen has no clue they're coming for her," Harvey suggested.

Terry agreed and they ran to the opposite side of the mountain. The stone pillars made a sort of half circle, with the center temple being almost inaccessible without using the bridges that had been constructed in the previous decade. Before then, the only way to get to the temples had been a series of rope ladders. Strong was glad for the improvements.

Strong knocked on the door to the first temple. A small monk answerd and smiled at them.

Terry mustered a hackneyed Greek sentence and the monk nodded his head. He motioned for them to enter and Terry pulled Strong inside. After they were out of view of the monk, Terry's walk turned into a full run and they were through the temple and onto the next bridge.

"What did you tell him—the monk?"

"I tried to say we were colleagues of Ellen Thatcher. I'm not sure if that's what I said, but it worked," Terry replied.

As they entered the next temple, Strong looked around and noticed the lavish artwork that decorated the walls of the temples. Some of the works probably dated to a century ago or more. He wondered if the world was aware at the treasures these temples contained. To his surprise, there weren't many monks present inside the temples. It was as if they had become part of the temples themselves and were not separate entities any longer.

Terry burst through the rear door of the second temple and onto the bridge across to the next. Strong caught sight of the group across the other side. At that same moment, the man in the gray suit turned and spotted them as well. He pointed to Strong and Terry and the group of guards closest to him started shooting at them. Strong dove to the ground and saw Terry do the same. They dog-crawled to the entrance of the centermost temple and then burst through the doors. Inside, a few monks fled to rooms within the temple. Terry jumped up and ran to the other door, barring it shut and pulling a large wooden piece of furniture in front of it.

Strong slowly got up. "Damn, I'm tired of getting shot at."

To his left, a brown-haired woman got up from behind an overturned desk. She looked at Strong and her eyes widened in recognition.

"Harvey Strong?" Ellen Thatcher's gasp revealed her disbelief.

"Ellen?"

"What are you doing here? Who is shooting at the temples?"

"Look—I can't explain at the moment. The important part is that there's a group of men outside with guns. Where can we go?"

"Uh, I guess the vaults below," said Ellen.

Strong looked down to the floor. "The vaults?"

"The temples all have vaults built into the stone. The temples are simply here to provide shelter to the monks that study and guard the contents," Ellen explained.

At that moment, there came a bang on the rear door. Men shouted and prepared to bust it down.

"All right," Strong urged. "Lead the way."

Ellen led Strong and Terry to a room within the temple. A monk was inside, but he ran out when they appeared. She motioned for Strong to help her move a table across the room. After it was cleared, Ellen pulled back the rug and revealed a trap door in the floor. Strong was shocked, but it wasn't the first secret he had ever run across in his career. Ellen opened it up and motioned for them to get in. Strong went first, followed by Terry, and finally Ellen, who shut the door behind her and pulled the lock shut.

"That lock will buy us some time, but they'll get in eventually," she warned.

"Where the hell are we gonna go?" Terry looked around anxiously.

Inside was a ladder that led them to a vast expanse beneath the temple. It must have taken hundreds upon hundreds of years for the monks to carve away at the stone. Inside were narrow alleyways and cubby holes in the rock. Ellen walked down one of the alleyways and the Strong brothers followed her.

"Unfortunately," Ellen directed her words toward Terry. "There isn't anywhere to go. This vault is not for retreating. It's for safeguarding."

"What do they keep down here?" Strong asked.

"Only the monks truly know. As a scholar, they give me limited access to the artifacts. I've been trying to earn their trust for the past few months." Ellen turned down a corner and lead them into a cubby hole. It seemed like she knew where she was going. "Actually, I have to thank you. Without that distraction up there, it may have been years before I was allowed down here."

"What are you looking for, Ellen?" Strong asked. "And why aren't you at home, in England?"

"I was in a school studying ancient texts. Some translated Greek text led me here in search of an artifact."

"A key?" Terry suggested, recalling what Campbell had said.

"How do you know?" Ellen stopped at a small cubby hole in the stone. There was no door, but the entrance to the compartment was smaller than a typical entrance to a room. After all, carving stone was no easy task.

Ellen ducked and walked into the compartment. Strong and Terry did the same. Inside, Ellen lit a small candle on the wall to her left. The candle flame illuminated the small room and revealed a small box sitting on a table in the center. The box was plain, but was obviously well made. It looked like cherry to Strong. It had a large, golden lock on the front.

"Yes, a key," Ellen told Terry. She turned to Strong, saying, "Do you remember in Quebec when I fell down in that hole in the cave?"

Strong nodded and she continued, "Well, before you helped me out, I grabbed this key."

Ellen pulled a large dagger from beneath her shirt. It was gilded and had what looked like the teeth of a key on the bottom. It was held to her neck by a gold chain.

"I never told anyone, frankly, because I forgot about it with all the Nazis and shooting going on. When I returned to England, I focused my studies on finding out what in the hell this key was for. Well, after the Norse mythologies yielded nothing, I turned my gaze to those places that Vikings had raided. Turns out, Leif Erikson and his crew made a raid in northern Scotland before their trek to Greenland. Anything they took from that area would have been in their plunder they buried in Quebec. So, I turned to the Scottish histories. Luckily, Scotland was close to home, so my dad didn't worry about me."

"So where does Greece come in?" Strong was getting impatient. Suddenly, there was gunfire above them. Strong worried about the monks who were caught in the crossfire.

"Well, as you may guess, Greece and Scotland don't have much in common. However, there is a small anecdote about a Greek emissary that visited the British Isles in the early part of the second millennia. It is said that he was a trader and that he was close with the family of a blacksmith there. No more mention of him is made. So I tracked this man's history back to Glyfada. That's when I set sail last year. I told my dad I was doing a missionary trip."

"And?" Terry blurted out. "What did you find? Why here?"

"A key?" Terry asked.

"Patience," Ellen smiled. "But anyways, I found mention of the Cult of the Builder, who is revered by blacksmiths and craftsmen for…"

Strong interrupted. "We are well aware the Builders. Skip to the key."

"All right, well, the key is to this box. The Greek trader who visited Scotland stole the key in the early 1000s and made sure the Cult of the Builder would never find it again. What's in this box I do not know, but it takes this key." Again, Ellen held it up.

"I think we may be able to fill in that blank," suggested Strong. Another round of gunfire came and then a consistent pounding above them. Men were trying to get into the vault.

Strong relayed the story of the necklace and the man who wanted it back, Anagnos. "I think we are in the middle of a war we have no business being in. Ellen, we need to give them the key and go home."

"No!" Said Ellen and Terry in unison.

Terry spoke up, "We can't give in, Harvey. They have my wife, for God's sakes. I'm not gonna give in to them. Besides, they won't just let us go after all we've done to impede their mission."

"He's right," Ellen agreed. "Everything I've found on this Cult of the Builder is bad news. They don't play games and they don't leave witnesses. The Greek trader who stole the key he died for his actions."

Suddenly, a burst came through overhead and the trio heard the shouts of the men entering the vault down the narrow alleyway.

As Strong and Terry peered out of the cubby hole and down the alleyway, Ellen used the key to open the box. When Strong looked back, she was holding a large, golden necklace in front of her. The amulet at the bottom looked as it shined without light. It was a mixture of blue and green. Ellen stared at it for what seemed like forever. Finally, she placed it around her neck and tucked it under her shirt.

As Strong took another look down the alleyway, he caught a glimpse of two armed guards carrying torches. They spotted him and opened fire with their guns. He ducked his head back in and pulled the Webley Mark VI from his waistband. Terry pulled the Colt 1911 from his and racked the slide.

"All right, Ellen, stay back as far as you can until we say otherwise. There's at least six or more of them and they're all armed," ordered Strong. She nodded.

Terry adjusted the pistol in his hands. "They might have Amara out there. Be careful of what you're shooting at."

With their guns cocked and ready to go, Strong and Terry jumped out from the compartment and began firing. One of the men fell dead, but the other jumped behind a wall. Behind him, three more men were running toward them.

Strong fired too quickly and, after a moment, his gun was clicked on empty. He threw it down and dove behind a nearby wall. Terry kept firing, winging another attacker. He knelt down, aimed his pistol, and was suddenly struck by a bullet in the arm. He dropped the 1911 and fell to his back, grabbing at his injured shoulder. Strong pulled him to his side. He shushed his brother's groaning and then called out for Ellen to stay put.

Three guards came closer to their position until Strong could feel their heavy breathing and footsteps.

Suddenly, Ellen called out: "Stop! Please stop!"

The three guards stopped. Strong was confused on why they would heed the words of the woman they have been seeking so easily.

She cried out again: "Stop shooting at us. We are no harm to you. Drop your guns and leave."

The sounds of three rifles hitting the stone floor echoed in the vault. The footsteps of the three guards faded further and further away. After a moment, Ellen stepped out into the passageway.

The necklace glowed blue through her tan blouse as she was peering down the passageway. She had a puzzled look on her face. She shouted to Strong, "They're gone. They left! C'mon, let's go!"

Strong helped Terry off the floor and dragged him down the alleyway. The trio slowly made their way past the stone compartments and finally to the trap door. Strong went first and then helped Terry out. At the top, they were met with pistols pointed at their heads. Strong stopped moving and listened for orders. The guards leaving had been a trick to flush them out. He felt stupid.

Strong and Terry were led out of the room and through the temple by two guards holding pistols. The man in the gray suit walked behind them. He had a clean-shaven face and a menacing look to him. He did not smile or make a movement. As they exited the temple, Strong saw Amara and Campbell were being held hostage by two guards on the bridge. Strong and Terry were pushed alongside them.

"Shoot them all!" Ordered the man in gray. From behind him, in the temple door, Ellen appeared.

"No! You will not shoot them," she commanded forcefully. "You will drop your guns and leave, now!"

The two guards looked at each other and then dropped their weapons. They walked past the man in gray and entered the next temple. The other two guards holding Amara and Campbell were flabbergasted. The man in gray pulled a pistol of his own.

Ellen walked up to the bridge. She stood tall and stared at the man in gray. He stared at her and then smiled.

"You are lovely, m'dear," said the man in a Greek accent.

Ellen's eyebrow raised. She was stunned by the man's words. Strong, too, was in a state of confusion. He wanted to know what was going on.

"You're the loveliest creature to ever walk this Earth. I am your servant for all time," said the man.

Ellen looked down and saw the glow of the amulet on the necklace. She looked back up at the man in gray. She shook her head.

The man in gray touched Ellen's face and smiled again, saying, "Your command is my mission."

Amara gasped. "It's the Necklace of Harmonia."

"What?" Ellen queried.

"That necklace, it is the legendary Necklace of Harmonia. It entrances any man you speak to. They are your eternal slaves while you possess the necklace. The legend is true, after all," finished Amara.

Ellen quickly took off the necklace and threw it to the ground. "It also brings ruin to you and your house."

As Ellen removed the necklace, the man in gray quit smiling. The spell lifted from his mind and heart. He raised his pistol and pointed it at Ellen. The guards did to same to Strong and Terry.

Amara picked up the necklace and stared at it. She turned and rushed to the man in gray. He grabbed her and held her tightly, kissing her on the lips.

"What the hell is going on?" Terry shouted.

Amara turned to Terry, replying, "Oh, Terry, you stupid, stupid boy. Did you really think I would fall for some poor, American journalist? My father is wealthy. I have power beyond your imagining. I don't need you."

Terry's jaw dropped. Strong looked at his brother, and felt sorry for him.

"Then why marry me?"

"My father is a very powerful man," Amara answered. "He is Anagnos, leader of the Cult of the Builder. It is my destiny to wear this necklace."

Strong lowered his head. All this time, when it seemed they were running *from* Anagnos and the Cult, they were running *with* it. Amara had played both the Strong brothers for fools.

"I must thank you, though, Terry. When you became indebted to my father, he saw an opening to acquire the services of Harvey Strong, adventurer-extraordinaire. You fell for me so easily and, after I prodded you to have your brother at the wedding, it only took a little time to get him on board."

Amara turned to Ellen. "I must also thank you, Ms. Thatcher. I owe you mightily for helping us find the necklace. We thought the key was gone forever and, without it, the necklace, too."

"Screw you," Ellen displayed a bit of her father shining through. "You may have the necklace, but you won't for long."

"Honey, with this necklace, I cannot be stopped. It may be a man's world we live in, but with this I will command every man in it. They will not be able to resist me."

Amara slowly put the necklace around her neck and the amulet glowed. She turned to the guards holding Campbell and the Strongs prisoners.

"Jump off the bridge," ordered Amara.

The two guards looked at each and, in their eyes Strong could see that they wanted nothing more than to live. However, the power of the necklace was true. They dropped their rifles, hopped over the side of the bridge, and plummeted to their deaths thousands of feet below. Amara laughed like a young girl.

She grabbed Ellen in a chokehold and lifted her off her feet. It seemed the necklace also gave her unnatural strength.

Suddenly, gunfire commenced. From the temple behind them, a group of a dozen men appeared, guns blazing. At the front was Mack Thatcher, dual pistols firing as fast as they could. Strong smiled, remembering the telegram he had sent from the communications office to London. He knew it would take Mack some time to get here, but if Ellen was in trouble, he wouldn't hesitate.

Amara dropped Ellen to the ground as Strong, Terry, and Campbell grabbed whatever guns they could. The gunfire stopped once the man in gray and Amara raised their hands in defeat. Strong raised his gun and pointed it at Amara. He couldn't believe what was happening.

As Mack and his team slowly walked down toward the bridge, Amara yelled out, "No man here will harm me! No man here will fire his gun!"

At that moment, Mack raised a pistol and prepared to kill this woman who harmed his daughter. Only, he found himself unable to pull the trigger. He tried, with all his might, but could not do it. He struggled with the trigger, but then dropped the pistol into the dirt next to Ellen.

Amara laughed. "Don't you see, old man, you have no power over me. I am an unstoppable force. I can kill each and every one of you. Or have each of you kill each other."

With her last statement, she turned her attention to the Strong brothers.

"Both of you, walk over here to the edge of the cliff." Amara pointed to a bare spot on the stone pillar where there was no bridge or barrier.

"Terry, drop your weapon over the edge," she added. Unwillingly, Terry did so.

"Harvey, point your gun at your brother." Strong felt helpless. As his own hands raised the gun at Terry, he felt like his own will to live was gone. He was utterly helpless.

He looked at Amara, whose eyes were shining like a child playing with dolls. She was making these men do whatever she pleased. Strong had an uneasy feeling that it would become the last act he ever did.

"Now, shoot Terry in the head and send him falling to his death."

"No!" Strong used is immense strength of will to keep his own finger from pulling the trigger on the rifle. Terry's face was full of sadness, but he mustered a smile.

"Harvey, I forgive you. I know you would never hurt me."

"No!" Strong fought harder and harder to keep from killing his own flesh and blood. He remembered his father's last wish: "Protect your brother. Keep him safe."

Now, Strong was going to kill the person he had spent his whole life saving. His finger touched the edge of the trigger. Sweat poured down his face from struggling to avoid pulling the trigger. Suddenly, a gun fired.

Strong turned to see Amara's face white with shock. A bullet hole appeared in her chest and blood ran down her blouse. Behind her, Ellen held a smoking rifle.

Ellen walked up to Amara. She pulled the necklace off Amara and threw it down. With the necklace off, Strong's finger was released from its command and he dropped the rifle.

Ellen pointed the rifle at Amara and cocked the bolt smiling. "That necklace can control any man, sure. But I'm no man."

With her last word, Ellen fired the rifle and Amara's body was thrown backwards over the cliff's edge. Blood splattered on the man in the gray suit/ He took off running across the bridge. Terry turned, pointed his rifle, and dropped the man as he approached the temple door.

Ellen was looking down where Amara's dead body had disappeared as Mack approached her. He took the rifle from her hands and grabbed her tightly. She held her father close.

Strong grabbed Terry, too, and held him tightly.

"I'm sorry, Terry, I would never have…" whispered Strong.

"I know, Harvey, I know."

The temple monks appeared from their hiding places. One was carrying the box that the necklace belonged in. The monk slowly approached the necklace, lifted it from the dirt, and placed it inside the box. Another monk, who seemed to be the leader in the temple, was carrying the key to the box. He walked past Strong and Terry and approached Lachlan Campbell and handed him something before departing with his fellow monks.

"Why did that monk give you the key?" Asked Strong.

"A deal is a deal," Campbell related. "My ancestor was the Scot who traded with the Greek for this key. My family has safeguarded it for generations. Now,

I will take it home and continue that legacy."

"What did the Greek trader get?"

"One sheep," Campbell chuckled. "He just wanted the key as far away from Greece as possible."

Terry lowered his rifle and walked up to Ellen and Mack. Terry said hello to Mack, whom he had not seen in many years. Then, when Mack left to see Strong, Terry introduced himself formally to Ellen.

"I thought you were a goner," Terry smirked.

"I thought the same about you," she grinned. "Nice shooting."

"You too. Do you want to get food in the temple with me?"

"Aren't you a married man?"

"Not any more. Thanks to you."

Terry and Ellen then slung their rifles over their shoulders and entered the temple. Strong and Mack exchanged greetings and a quick hug.

"Harvey, why are you always writing to me for help?"

"Because all my other friends are dead or keep telling me I owe them money. I'm glad you made it. I almost shot my brother."

"Some best man you are."

After the crew recuperated from their terrifying experience, they loaded the bodies of the Cult of the Builder into the truck and left the monks to their work. It didn't take much convincing for Terry to leave his life in Greece behind and return to the world of the living. In London, Strong bid Campbell farewell as he boarded a train home to Scotland. Campbell hoped he could safeguard the key a bit better than his predecessors.

Strong, Mack, Terry, and Ellen made their way to the *Galloping Mare* for a final farewell and a drink to do so rightly. Strong showed Mack a picture of Cate holding their son Henry.

"Are you sure he's yours?" Joked Mack. "He's a bit better looking than I expected a Strong man to be."

"Yeah, I'm sure. He drives his mother crazy, just like his old man."

Strong couldn't wait to return home to New York. His literary agent would be fuming over his missed book tour stops. He would manage to win her over with a new manuscript about his latest adventure. Cate, too, would take some wooing to get back on her good side. He planned to take her and Henry to Coney Island the day he got home. Strong found it odd that now he only wished for things like an ice cream and a hug from his son. Guns, treasure, and adventure were for the young. He looked over at Terry and Ellen, who were laughing together in the corner.

"Don't speak ill of Strong men, Mack, you might be related to one, soon," he cautioned pointing to Terry.

Mack quickly moved from his seat to sit between Ellen and Terry. The next day, when Strong was loading his luggage into the taxi to make the trip to the airport, Terry revealed he would not be coming with him.

"Give my love to Cate and Henry, but I think I've got a new adventure brewing here." He looked back at Ellen.

Strong smiled and hugged his brother.

"Just make sure this one doesn't try to kill you," whispered Strong.

EPILOGUE - A MONTH LATER

"**S**ir, we've located your daughter's body," said a man wearing all black and carrying a pistol on his side. He laid a blood-stained blouse on the large, wooden desk.

The man behind the desk wore a fine gray silk suit. As he grabbed the blood-stained blouse, he removed his fedora and placed it on the desk. He puffed his cigar once and then smashed it into the top of the desk. Suddenly, he began pounding his fist into the top of the desk. He did so harder and harder until a dent was left in the wood.

For a moment, the man sat hunched over the blouse, his large chest sucking air in and out. Behind the desk, a painting of a large blacksmith forging something on an anvil stared down at him.

Anagnos looked up from his desk and into the eyes of the man standing in front of him. In a low, deep voice full of hatred and revenge muttered, "Find Harvey Strong."

THE END

OUR CREATORS

WRITER –

TYLER AUFFHAMMER - is the author of numerous works of fiction, nonfiction, and poetry, including 2018's *1950s Western Roundup* and 2021's *Marshal Horne of Talon's Crossing*. He lives in theAppalachian mountains with his family.

INTERIOR ILLUSTRATOR & COVER ARTIST

RON HILL - has been an editorial cartoonist, humorous illustrator, graphic designer, educator, author, armchair theologian and video documentarian (not all at the same time, of course!) for over 40 years. Born in Cleveland, he graduated from the Art Institute of Pittsburgh and immediately returned to Northeast Ohio to begin working in advertising.

In the 1980s–90s, as part of the illustration team of Lombardo & Hill, Ron drew countless interior illustrations for role-playing games published by TSR, West End Games, Iron Crown Enterprises, and Chaosium, many involving licensed from The Lord of the Rings, Dungeons and Dragons, Indiana Jones and Star Wars. An accomplished quick-sketch caricature artist, he has drawn (to date) probably a quarter-million faces at thousands of private and public events from Chicago to New York. His editorial cartoons have appeared in the *Chagrin Valley Times, Solon Times, Geauga Times Courier* and *West Life* since 1999. In 2000 he started illustrating the popular "Armchair Theologian" book series for Westminster John-Knox; these 15 volumes have been translated into German, Japanese, Korean, Portuguese and Italian.

From 2002–2015, he taught an Interactive Media College Tech Prep program at Alliance High School, and has always conducted workshops at area art centers (including the Valley Art Center) since 1990. After co-founding Act 3, a media company and indie publisher in Cleveland in 2016, he has recently embarked (once again) on his solo career as a freelance artist, and is also currently working on a number of personal documentary projects, including"Go-Kart Therapy" and "We Are Doc Savage: A Documentary on Fandom." He has always lived in the Chagrin Valley of Northeast Ohio, and you can learn more at www.RonHillArtist.com. He can be contacted and found here: ArtistRonHill@gmail.com RonHillArtist.com

THE LAW IN TALON'S CROSSING

Talon's Crossing, Nevada is a fast growing western town with its share of growing pains. Born on the edge of the frontier by ranchers and farmers weary of the horrors of the past Civil War, it is home to both the good and the bad. Men and women seeking their fortune off a land that doesn't give it up easily. From buffalo hunters, to miners, cattlemen and gunfighters, all contending with the desperate Indian tribes and the unforgiving weather.

Maintaining law and order in Talon's Crossing is veteran lawman Marshal Gideon Horne and his young, inexperienced Deputy Seth Barr. In four new stories they condend with an audacious shooting competition, the mysterious murder of a cowhand, a notorious outlaw gang on the loose and the discovery of gold in the surrounding hills.

With "Marshal Horne of Talon's Crossing," writer Tyler Auffhammer has recaptured the romantic adventure of classic western TV series ala "Gunsmoke" and "The Lawman" among many others. His stories evoke a time when the American West paved the road to a country's unstoppable future.

AN AIRSHIP 27 PRODUCTION

PULP FICTION FOR A NEW GENERATION!

AIRSHIP27HANGAR.COM

NEW PULP

www.ingramcontent.com/pod-product-compliance
Lightning Source LLC
Chambersburg PA
CBHW070822250626
47170CB00006B/2191

* 9 7 8 1 9 5 3 5 8 9 6 9 9 *